Death

Death
Andy N

Death was written between April 2011 and October 2024 and is @ Andy N (aka A.E. Nicholson). All rights are reserved. No reproduction, copy or transmission of this publication may be made without written permission. This book is a work of fiction, and the opinions displayed in this book are of the narrator only and the author has asserted his right to be identified as the authors of this work in accordance with the Copyright, Designs and Patents act 1988.

Andy

I know where and when exactly I died, almost as well as I know exactly when and where I was born.

I know when the sun rose for the first time when I was placed in my mother's arms and she looked at me amazed with a love that only a mother has like I know when was the last time I breathed out for the final time and fell to the ground knowing I was never going to walk through the meadows again with the sun on my back, let alone see my family or any of my friends ever again.

I know it was twelve minutes past twelve on the 28th of January in 2013 when I died like I know exactly how much cheese I had on my sandwich which I had eaten thirty minutes before like I know where I was born almost to the very second.

I was born say five to ten miles away in Park Hospital (now Trafford General Hospital) on the 27th of February in 1970 to Robert and Helen Nicholls, both of whom lived on Edge Lane on the borderline of Chorlton and Stretford and had two more children over the next few years after me, Lizzie and another Son, Bobby who was born nine years after me almost to the day and by chance almost to the very minute.

If you research me, you'll see I was/am the author of five full-length novels and two films, with a 6th one close to being completed and was the owner of Brown Accountants which I bought with the profits (yeah, lol) of the adaptation of my first novel after I eventually moved back to Chorlton.

You'll see also if you look around, my third novel 'Birth' talked about my indie band 'Siren' which I co-formed when I was 16, and which collapsed when I was around 18 after my girlfriend at the time, Tara cheated on me with our bass player, and I simply ran away from Chorlton (where I live) and travelled all over the UK until I came back to Chorlton for the first time in 15 years for Bobby (my brother)'s wedding and him and his now wife invited Tara along to the launch.

The rest I'll come onto next.

On the day I died, I stepped out of our home to head to work, I stupidly decided I wouldn't need my coat thinking I would be okay for a little brisk walk only to then turn back after less than a few moments when the wind decided to start violently laughing in my face.

I then made the same mistake also at lunch when I died when I decided to go out minus my coat not realising how chilly it was and ended up making a sharp exit back to the office, only to then start regretting it the closer I got to where I died again.

I remember when the sun came back out walking past the side of the Horse and Jockey, I looked at the clouds breaking and then the breeze suddenly cut off, I thought I don't bloody believe it, and threw my coat over my back and thought I would have to put up with it, only for the coat to at least partly protect me when I hit the floor,

But not enough to save me from dying as it turned out.

Since I took over the accountants when I moved back to Chorlton for good, I always made sure I went for a walk past the old gate that led to the back of the Old Factory. as often as I could every lunch, time permitting.

My Grandmother, who I barely knew truth be told I always remember telling me as a child not to go near there, "It's evil, that's place Andy" She would say to me and both my brother and sister at the nursing home where she eventually died constantly whenever I would tell them where I had been walking after School.

"Mum" Our Mum I always remember would frequently cut in, trying to stop her from carrying on.

"Helen" She would carry on "You know I am telling you, there was always something evil about that place, I'll stand by it that until the very day I die."

Truth be told, without Grandmother telling us, I likely would have never gone near it, but she sparked off my interest, and from about 12 to 14, I used to wander around the outskirts of it constantly after School.

Of course I never told my parents I went around it, but I never saw anything and all I saw was a deserted old building.

I never felt the evil around there that grandmother claimed, although considering I died not far from there, God knows what everybody else would have felt afterwards.

Work had been manic looking back at things after a rush order that came in from a bar up the road which got hit by its shareholders who wanted a complete audit like yesterday.

The job I knew had come into ourselves the day before and as soon as I saw the size of the job, I said to both Gordon and Sandra my two main assistants 'I hope you don't have any plans for the weekend as I think this is going to wreck both of your plans, and mine also'.

Gordon and Sandra had been working for me for a good number of years coming in almost straight after I took over the accountants, and I liked them both hugely almost like they were actual family.

Gordon who I hired first out of the pair of them was a shy, timid grey-haired Scotsman in his early 50s and the day after he started, when the other person I also hired didn't turn up, I always remember him saying "One of my neighbors is good, reliable, she can help out for a few days until you er.. get somebody else in".

She, Sandra came around the day after, and I ended up taking her on Permanent less than two weeks later, a retired English teacher who was looking for some extra work to help her top up her pension and used to act like a second mother to me, making sure I ate every day and went outside for a short break.

"Come on, Andy" She would always say to me just turned 12.30 every day "Isn't it time for your walk?".

I felt guilty that day, I have to be honest, felt guilty about that last-minute job that came out, but I couldn't afford really to turn it down, and the guys, both of them knew that, but they also knew I would look after when it was out of the way with a little bonus, not necessarily on the books of course.

It was none of my business with either Gordon or Sandra, you could easily say they were just lifelong friends (which they were) if you ever came into the office, and they didn't know that I knew, but they had also been secretly seeing each other for at least the last eighteen months despite the fact they were both seeing somebody else technically, and I knew they both would be heartbroken when they heard how I died.

I had rung up Tara (More on that shortly) just before I left the office and had heard both of the girls (More on that also soon) whisper bye to me.

"Neither of them in college today"? I remember saying to Tara.

"Nope, their lecturer today has a stomach upset today and wants them to all work from him researching Plato"

"Ouch," I laughed at her hanging up remembering how much I hated him back when I was their age.

Even though when they were both 17, soon to be 18 and they were both amazingly clever in each of their personal ways, they were both still nightmares trying to get them out of bed they had to be in college in the morning.

Both of them were both good girls and hadn't caused neither me nor Tara a lot of trouble since we got together and were both doing brilliantly at college and were both certs for good grades when they got to their final exams.

Both of them were however rubbish at getting up in the morning and the least said about both going to bed at the time Tara wanted them to go to bed (I kept out of that as much as possible as I wasn't that biological father) the better which usually ended up being a constant battle.

Considering they were both nearly women when I died, we would never try to push them into going to bed, but I know they would sometimes use me as an excuse for not going to bed at the time ("You and Andy don't go to bed until god knows what time, why should we?) when Tara tried to drop hints they would struggle the following day if they didn't go to bed at a reasonable hour, but right up to those final few days before I died it just seemed work seemed to keep building up and up with my agent on the phone with more little minute edits on my novel from my publishers.

Kelly who had been my agent for ten years and had been responsible for the higher and higher advances I had been receiving for my last two books was rightly furious when she rang me up just when I was just getting ready to head on for my walk from the office saying "I think what they are asking for here is bang out of order here, Andy with this latest round of edits".

"It's okay" I groaned slightly.

This book in question I am going to talk about had not been an easy book to write and had resulted in more than four more complete massive redrafts than what either of my previous two novels had gone through.

"Legally, you could tell them to get stuffed here" She carried on, "I don't see why they are asking you to make those changes"

I nearly didn't answer Kelly and just looked at the Clock.

She was dead right.

"One of those things," I answered after a few seconds pause and then mumbled softly which only she would hear "Bastards".

"I think I could get you more at York and York and you would have not got half of the hassle we have been getting here with these boys". She carried on.

I put my coat on "Forward over to me the email over to me that they have sent to you, and I'll have a look over the weekend, I promise. We've had a last-minute audit come in, but I'll do my best"

"I'm sorry to be ruining your weekend" She apologised again for the hassle she was causing me.

"It's okay, it's one of those things" I sat down and looked down at the floor for a few seconds when I eventually put the phone down before then started swearing a few times repeatedly softly.

This wasn't Kelly's fault as soon I told myself as soon as I stepped out of the office and slowly walked past the Horse and Jockey towards St Clements Road towards home, it wasn't her fault atall, I knew from working with her for so many years she would have argued the toss with them until she would have told them where to stick it but it didn't mean I liked it still.

Tara would have seen as soon as I got home and left me to it that it was going to be one of those weekends when I would barely move from the study again and before I knew it the weekend would have flown by, and I would have still been in the middle of it by the time it was going to head back to the day job on Monday.

I know the latest draft of my Manuscript is all over the place in my study minus the corrections that the publishers wanted, which I hadn't seen but which I honestly dreaded walking down to the Woods that day but I nearly to clear my head.

I suspect what they wanted me to do was unreasonable and looking back at it now, I generally was surprised that they accepted it in the first place.

"I can't believe they've accepted it" I remember Kelly telling me about a few days before Christmas the year before I died "They think it could easily end up being a massive seller"

I was stunned, as were both Tara and both girls when I told them.

"That's serious money," Tara said to me stunned "That's serious, serious money, are you sure about this?"

I didn't know honestly, my previous novels had all done well, well average to good in some cases, so was a little unsure, but we agreed to go for it, and see how it went.

It's immaterial now of course. All I can say is I was planning to return it that night after work to spend another hour or two on it and do what I could over the weekend in between what I had on that audit then the night after that and probably the next few nights after that to try and get it into some kind of steady order of what I needed to do next etc.

It could have been a good novel, probably my best book so far if I hadn't died, but we'll never know now.

Hopefully, between both Tara and Kelly, they would be able to work out what I had planned for the final draft and would choose to respect my wishes and publish the book even if it was for litigation reasons at worst and at best get her a couple of thousand pounds at least to give Tara and the girls some breathing space to sort out what the heck they were going to do next.

Tara knew the password to my laptop and would access the manuscript on their easily enough but then would have to deal with my handwritten corrections scattered over the place on the printed-off version.

I know my handwriting wasn't great at the best of times, but I would hope between both of them that they would be able to work exactly what I had scribbled down and once they had done that hopefully the publishers would just give up arguing out of respect for what happened to me and publish it.

I know of some people whose family never meet their agents, but as soon as it looked Tara and I looked we were going places a couple for the second time, I made sure Kelly, and her wife came up from London and met them.

It helped a lot here in this case that Kelly's Mum lived just up the road in Didsbury around the back of the clock tower which is only about a fifteen-minute drive from us, so it gave me the excuse the first time I could arrange it she was up to pop over to see me also for a meeting at ours, and then we went and met Tara and the girls at the Horse and Jockey afterwards.

Hand on my heart, I don't recall how well they got on that afternoon but I do remember that after that meeting whenever Kelly rang me up at home and spoke to Tara or one of the girls before me, they would laugh at something or the other before eventually passing the phone over to me.

Before I met Kelly, I had had a few other agents mostly down London way when I lived down that way which made life easier when I lived down there (Less so when I lived both in Liverpool and Blackpool) and I don't like being horrible when I say simply didn't have my interests really at heart, and if I hadn't been alert would have caused no end of trouble with my first book, and then the book of short stories I had published two years after that.

Kelly and her team were the complete opposite I found straight from the beginning when I first met her, friendly, honest, and of course after a nice financial package but wanted it in a way that suited me as well as them.

I remember her telling me when we first met a week after she read the second draft of what became my first novel "The Unspoken"

"I know about three publishers who would snap this up" She began.

"Really" I looked at her stunned.

"Yes" She learned forward slightly "And most of them I wouldn't touch with a barge pole for you here" and I knew without answering her then she had my best interests at heart.

When I stumbled into becoming a novelist in my mid-20s, I never had had any big thoughts I would make it big and just hoped it would provide a nice, steady additional income and allow me to work part-time in some office but I would have let my work remain unpublished than be published rather than what some of the deals that one of these so-called agents tried to get me to accept.

To this day, I don't know how Kelly got the deal for me like she did with my third novel, my first book of non-fiction 'Birth 'which talked about the birth of my writing and hope I first met Tara and formed a rock band which nearly made turned into a good steady seller and left to higher and higher advances for the following three books which allowed me to buy a house in Chorlton Cum Hardy almost outright within months of when I eventually returned to live in the area.

Even if they manage to get this novel published, if Tara and both of the girls wanted to Kelly to do so, there is more work unpublished on my laptop, a nearly finished novella that I was planning to wrap once I got this novel finished, a good book of poetry or two and all kinds of bits of freelance journalism, copywriting and some non-fiction which I dare if there was the demand that they could draft into a book or two of there was the demand which could help her in the years following my death.

I know Tara the night before I died would have not wanted me to worry about both girls, but I knew whether she was aware of this fact or not. I knew what was going on even without her telling me she was having problems with both and as I lay on the ground never to ever get back up again knew full well knew they would both be okay.

Kelly would look after them financially if Tara agreed with it.

All three of them would be okay and the girls would look after their mum as best emotionally as they could after I died even though they were quite young still.

It's a shame really as I know I would be unable to write any of the other books I had in mind after my current book.

I know Kelly was excited about two of the outlines I had emailed her only a few weeks before I died.

One of them is a spoof about what happened to somebody I knew in London which I generally was surprised which Kelly liked as I did it over a glass or two of wine over two or three days. (It's genius I remember her email the morning after)

The other Tara thought seriously I was joking about it when I told her about it. "I hope you are joking about that".

I wasn't and her face when I told her that was a picture when I told her, the idea came from during a short trip to Paris we'd both had a few weeks together when the girls were both away camping with Claire, Tara's sister and their family.

I shook my head "Nobody will know" smiling "They say write what you know"

"But we are not sure whether that couple were having an affair" Tara countered shocked after I had told her about it "It could be something innocent"

I shook my head, "Henceforth why I am moving it to London instead of Paris"

It's a shame that the book will never get written, as I had all kinds of plans for the book which are pointless explaining, but I could have taken them literally anywhere and I mean anywhere, and it could have led into the next twenty or thirty years or whatever instead of just staying in the back of my thoughts.

It hurts me looking back that I'll never know what would happen if Tara had rang me up at lunchtime straight after I had finished getting stressed out at both work and then about my novel.

I know she would carry regrets for years afterwards that she didn't call me or even pop round to the office or even text me to say love you and see you later leaving me to then simply go for a walk onto the meadows and walk into the gates of death.

I don't hold it against her for not bothering or simply forgetting last minute, but I would have died if not then somewhere along the line before her and both girls one way or the other I know in hindsight would have been left heartbroken.

Ever since I was a child, I knew I wouldn't make it to a ripe old age. I never knew exactly where I had got it from, I first came out with it when I was about 10 or 11, and had Mrs. Jenkins, my teacher telling everybody jokingly to just ignore me and then tell me off privately afterwards I shouldn't be talking about that.

"It's the truth" I always remember telling me "I won't live to your age, Mrs. Jenkins".

As it turned out, I was two years older than she was then when I died.

I was a strange kid I guess, only to then gained all kinds of weirder ideas about life and death the older I got.

For example, I have had always had this philosophy that all of our lives whether we have lived once or twice before or more our lives are lined up like a set of dominos which get knocked down one after the other slowly with everything pre-arranged from the very moments we were all born right up until whatever happens next and I believe I was destined to die then whether it was there or indeed right in front of her and the girls.

I don't need to overstate things, but it would go without saying I would miss her and both of the girls and I know she would be reduced to little more than a bundle of tears when somebody arrived and told her what had happened to me.

I know I would have been the same in reverse if something had happened to her and would be standing there with both of the girls in a total state of complete and utter shock.

I know she would rush around to her sisters around the corner and Claire would get her oldest, Amanda, to go and pick up both of the girls from school when she would sit there shocked with grief that would leave all of them completely shocked, simply shocked.

It's a funny thing in hindsight with Claire that she only came into her life when she was in her 30s. Danny, her adopted brother, I knew from when both I and Tara were in a band with him when we were in our teenage years (Danny's case 21) which nearly made it big.

In Claire's case it was completely different as she or Danny and indeed me in a slightly different way were simply aware of her existence right up to one night after work, I came home to Tara telling me she had received this strange Facebook message from a woman querying if she was related to Frank Nell and thought they could be sisters.

Frank, she told me she had found out some years after he died before I knew her, had been a bit of a ladies' man to put it simply and had women up and down England during his job as a truck driver, but a half-sister, she was left stunned.

I get messages all the time from people saying they were my children, I remember telling her joking.

But they are after your money she smiled but I believe her before then showing me a picture she had emailed her, and was stunned as they did look alike.

A lot.

"I don't believe it" She said to me stunned.

"She could still be a con merchant" I tried reasoning "She could be after all of your money"

"What money?" She tried making light of her previous comments.

"Either of our monies then" I corrected myself and we both laughed about it but she knew I was right to be worried and after ringing Danny who was on tour with his band in London said he didn't know anything about it either ended up meeting her in Didsbury Village when she came to Manchester two weeks later with her eldest daughter.

I told her I was uneasy about it, very uneasy about it but she was determined to meet her. Danny nearly dropped everything to come and meet us too, only for me to stop him and explain to him to carry with his tour adding "If it's true, we'll sort find out and can arrange for you to meet with her afterwards".

"Tara," She said, an attractive-looking lady with mouse brown hair arrived a few minutes after we did "You must be her husband, Andy. I've read your last novel. I thought it was pretty good".

I smiled, thanking her, and went to the bar to get her all a few drinks, thinking I could see what Tara had said about the pair of them looking alike for the first time and by the time I got back, her daughter Amanda had arrived after getting delayed a little finding somewhere to park.

Any doubts I may have had about Claire vanished when Amanda arrived swearing about how shite the parking was out there shortly after Claire did.

Now she really, really did look like Tara right from her nose to the way she bit her lip when she got nervous and when I got back from the bar with a drink for Amanda also, the three of them were already in a heated, completely unprintable conversation about what a total bellend and git Claire's ex-husband was like.

I left them and sat there talking to Kelly on the telephone on the other side of the bar.

"You couldn't make it up, honestly" I began.

Kelly laughed "Is she okay?"

"Two peas from the same pod" I paused.

"You'll probably barely see her again after this" She carried on shocked.

"We'll see" I paused listening to the three of them talk and by the time I went back on there a few minutes, I knew they were going to be a part of our lives whether any of us realised it or not.

Danny rang me up the following day at lunch when I was walking past the Horse and Jockey

"I cannot believe this" He started instead of any kind of greeting.

"Let's just see I am as shocked as you are mate" I looked towards the meadows slightly "I am not sure who is the more stunned out of the pair of us"

"You never knew Frances" He stumbled "And I can't say I knew him that long also before he buggered off, Nan always said he had more than a slight a wandering eye but another daughter, Jesus..." His swearing dropped off the line. "I'll be back tomorrow".

"She's already gone back to Birmingham" I finished off "But I think they said they will be seeing each other soon, so we can sort something out. I think you'd like her, Dan, her daughter, Amanda is the spit of Tara".

Despite what Kelly thought and also myself to a degree, Claire over the next few months moved from Birmingham with both of her girls (Amanda, and Diane) and a young boy (Paul) bought a house on the next road to us and the pair of them became the best of friends rapidly almost like they were making up for lost time and were a regular fixture at our house when I got back from the day job.

Danny I believe went over to Birmingham during some off time from his band and met her as soon as he could the week after I seem to recall and by the time Claire and her family relocated her family near to us, although the three of them hadn't met all in person, at least they all were aware of each of them, they all had talked which was a good start and all became closer over the next few months.

I'm glad Claire is living around the corner after all of this. I knew she wouldn't just sit there and not do anything and would take action to just keep things moving as much as she could as she knew Tara would simply go to pieces understandably when she had been told I had been found dead by the riverside.

Tara wouldn't, well actually none of them couldn't have guessed what would come next and Claire would say to her, they would get the person responsible for what has happened here even though she would know deep down it would be as much chance of it happening as finding a needle in a bloody haystack.

While Claire would be dealing with Tara, I knew she would have rung up Amanda at her work and she would have told her boss she was going to finish early finish urgently for the day to go and help out her mother.

I'd met her boss at the cleaners, Maggie once when they pressed my suit before I went over to London to meet up with some director from the BBC over some freelance script writing and knew without even worrying about it, she would let Amanda go quickly and pick up and look after both girls.

I know both girls were almost women, but they were still too young to deal with what was going to happen next.

Back when I was alive, I used to think my life was nothing out of the ordinary even though I worked part-time as a writer and general creative person and pre-Tara used to think nobody would miss me when I was gone, the reality is now looking back at my life I know the reality is very much different from the way Amanda alone would have dealt with the situation when her mum would have rung her up and her boss, Maggie even though I barely knew her.

Death, and a sudden, unexpected death like what happened to me affects people in funny ways from a simple that's horrible to read to the case of

Amanda who was a good, practical young lady who would pick up both of our girls from college.

I know Amanda would have gone into their college and spoken to whoever was in their Reception and got them quietly and made no fuss and got them back to Tara and Claire would have filled them in as briefly and to the point as she could.

I know Amanda would have then got both of her siblings around with the same amount of total loss of fuss and then rang up her stepdad, Frank who I'll come onto shortly.

She had the same matter-of-factness as Claire had, and I liked the fact that she was also considering doing a Master's degree at Manchester University in Creative Writing.

I'm not saying that I influenced her or anything about doing it, but she was certainly good enough to do it and was in the middle of her debut novel, which I think was very, very promising indeed and was as capable and as thoughtful as anybody you can have hoped to meet.

I wouldn't have to imagine what she would to both of the girls after seeing one of her friends at the Lloyds when she turned up for lunch with me and Tara and said with a little smile with two little girls I had never seen before "Becca's had to pop over to see her Mum in Hulme and asked me could I look after Melissa and Charlie until she got back" and looked after them with us like they were her younger sisters.

I know both of the girls were on the border of becoming young women, but I don't need to imagine what they would be like when they heard what had happened to me.

When Amanda had moved here with Claire, she ended up doing her sixth form at the School and a good chunk of the same teachers were still there and had told both me and Frank (her step-dad) she had seen on at least one occasion, she had seen Mr. Jenkins, the headteacher half cut at the Horse and Jockey with both of the girls and kept both of the girls from saying something at School the week after with cakes or biscuits, something that I and Tara certainly wouldn't have approved off if he had knew of it then.

If both girls had been a little younger, I know she would done the same calling it at Patel's around the corner with likely some kind of large cake or ice cream until Claire came back round to get them all to take them to Tara who would tell them both the bad news.

She did something similar I do remember when I became Diabetic a few years before that and got rushed into hospital after collapsing at work and tried to keep the girls distracted until Tara could get back from the hospital and be calm enough to deal with them and both me.

Of course, dying is a completely different ball game from becoming Diabetic and I know the best thing here would have been to get back home as quickly as possible.

I don't know what Tara would tell them exactly, I mean how on Earth do you tell two young ladies who loved their stepdad had been dead not far from his works near the river on Beech Road possibly beaten to death?

I know she would want time to try and explain to them why I wasn't coming back that night (which I know she would know I would completely agree with what I was saying, which I would if it had been her on the other side of the coin).

I know for a fact Claire would have run up Frank, her second husband, as soon as she could after Amanda had rung him up like I know for a fact as soon as she had heard something had happened to me.

Frank would have dropped everything whether his manager liked it or indeed not as the case may have been when Amanda then Claire rang him and pegged it out of the site he had been working on the corner of St. Clements Road.

I don't doubt also in addition he would also have gone straight over to the Scene of the Crime where he died demanding answers from whomever he was overseeing what was going on and full well known for a fact that wouldn't have taken no for an answer if they tried fobbing him off.

In some ways, I wish I would have been alive still to see what Frank would have said to them if they had tried

If I had still been there, I wouldn't have envied anybody trying to stop him then when he arrived and they then tried stopping him from getting to my body. I remember when his brother committed suicide, a good 18 months before he was eventually the same when he arrived at his flat only to be greeted by two Police Officers who advised they couldn't let him in.

Claire, I remember well ringing me asking if I could get over there as she was terrified of what he was going to do, he was going to hit one of the Policemen who were blocking the entrance of his brothers' house.

"He's my brother, damn it" He grumbled at me when the first of the two officers told him that they were going to be unable to grant us into what had being until just before had being his house.

"And unless you want to join him, I would let them do their job" I began in reply.

"We could arrest you alone for that comment" One of them answered a little shocked.

I couldn't blame him and for a good few moments, I honestly thought he would barge past them no matter what I or indeed would they say until they just moved out of the way and let us through.

"How the fuck do I think if he had any enemies?" I remember him when we were standing in the middle of his flat.

I shrugged my shoulders and tried smiling "He's your brother, I barely knew him"

He laughed and patted me on the back slightly looking around the flat "True, he was a miserable sod at the best of times and drunk way, way too much".

In my case, I know he would ask the same way as what happened to his brother as me.

I wouldn't say we were the best of friends after he got together with Claire and her family after they moved to the Chorlton area, but he always had my respect for the way he helped Claire bring up her two daughters and son in a way not too dissimilar to what happened between Tara and me.

I met Charlie once I think, maybe twice in hindsight when he came along to pick up the children to take them out for a meal in the Lloyds to which Frank told me stood just out of his earshot "He's a total waste of space".

I looked at him without answering. I knew the type, and could see from it without speaking to him, he was a thug and a bully

He told me an hour or so later in the Horse and Jockey watching him feed the three kids "The best thing for the three of them is he did a runner shortly after they were all born".

"Sounds a total charmer" I nodded in agreement.

"He has shown no interest in them since they were born" He paused, barely holding his tempter together "I'm amazed he bothers coming up honestly, if you look at the way he treats those kids there".

"I don't get you, he's paying their lunch"

"No, you don't get it, do you?" He changed tact "Look at his body language"

"He's not interested in them, well not interested in them"

He was right too. His heart was not in it.

"Last time I heard was in Watford, shacked up with some Rich widow or something. God knows how he did"

I nodded.

"He's probably only up here as she's probably threatening to throw him out or something"

I laughed slightly.

"This one is a Muppet fair enough" Frank put his beer down "But Charlie, dear, dear, dear you poor bastard" He went back to the bar.

Charlie, yeah, well he was completely right there as Charlie (that was his name), the father of both of Tara's girls last time I heard lived on one of the roads at the back of Longford Park and hadn't bothered trying to demand access for ages since Tara and I had started dating again.

This doesn't mean we hadn't seen around which I'll come onto later, but he had simply given up trying to bully Tara into letting him see the girls whenever he wanted, not when was good for her or indeed the girls since I came onto the scene.

After I died, I know Frank would have called round to make sure anyhow just to make sure Charlie's mucky fingerprints were involved in what happened to me.

If I was still alive, I would have told him, but Frank would have gone just to be safe rather than sorry in his eyes with a little reminder to make the little weasel didn't get any ideas now I was gone.

After that, Frank would have then I know without even having to hazard a guess would have gone round to see Bobby next as he lived across the road around the back of Stretford Grammer.

I'll talk about Bobby shortly, but Frank would know from talking to the Police that Bobby would have had nothing to do with my death but would want Bobby to know he was needed to step up to help Tara no matter what our relationship had been like over the last twenty years or so.

If he didn't already about what had happened from Tara or indeed Claire, he would soon find it was as much my fault as much as Bobby's or indeed the rest of my family how fragmented it had been for over twenty years after I first split from Tara and didn't return until I launched my third novel in the old bookshop opposite the Lloyds.

He would find if he didn't know already when we had first started talking properly in the months before "Birth" my novel was released, our relationship had been hesitant, almost nervous, but after I eventually moved back to Chorlton six months fully after I started dating Tara again, the distance or time had made it impossible to overcome and we eventually became little more than nodding acquaintances over the next few years only ever seeing each other at weddings, parties and funerals, the usual kind of thing.

I can't and won't blame Bobby for this as it was as much me as him what happened, if I had stayed, I am not sure whether things would have happened the way they did anyhow.

At College, I knew of two brothers Richard and Peter who were only 10 months apart in age and ended up in the same year in a lot of the classes I was in and simply did not get on.

Speaking personally, I really liked Richard even though he smoked way too much, of you know what, but there was always something weird about Peter and if I sensed it, I know for a fact Richard certainly did and had as little to do with him as possible.

I remember one time when we went to a pub just before I moved away from Chorlton when I was 18, and about six of us from college went to a pub on the edge of Didsbury which I have forgotten the name of looking back but had a massive room full of huge pool tables.

One of the lads we were, Baz or something played bass with another band which were certainly going places, much more than Siren was (and was not shy in telling me that either) and had a well-paid gig coming up supporting somebody in Stockport the night after and starts messing around with arm wrestling while a little drunk just to show how strong he was.

He said to me "Come on Andy, you're a big strong lad, you'll have a good chance against me, loser buys a beer".

I smiled gently declining despite the fact I was tall and lanky then; I wasn't particularly strong "Nah" I shook my head "You'll murder me Baz" and slowly walked back to our Pool table.

Before Baz could say anything further to me, Peter however jumped in saying "I'll do it, I'll do it".

Baz shrugged his shoulders almost to say why not and Peter locked arms with him only to twist Baz's wrist in a little more than a few seconds and leave Baz howling on the floor in pain.

I stood there shocked; I didn't know what to say as did the rest of the lads who were out, but Richard was furious.

I'd never seen him so angry with anybody as he was so easy-going it was scary and he leapt on him and it took three of us to pull him off from trying to really physically hurt him and he refused to get in a taxi with him and made him walk all the way home.

None of us knew what to say.

He wasn't our brother or anything, I wasn't going to argue with him, and I don't know how long it took for him to get home.

We saw them both in college the week after, but they weren't speaking.

I couldn't blame Richard there.

I don't recall seeing either of them much after that, but the relationship between them does remind me of the way things went between me and Bobby, just not when we were 17 or 18 but many, many years later.

I don't know who was right or who was wrong with both Richard and Peter looking back, perhaps it was a case of Peter being well out of order or perhaps it was Richard's fault or a combination of both of their faults or it was just one of those things.

Either way, I never saw either of them after that night out I have to admit but the scars of that night stung me for the next twenty years after I went to university and never really returned.

Unlike Richard and Peter who probably blamed each other for that night, what ruined their relationship between me and Bobby was simply when I walked away from my family, and I know that.

I know from talking to Bobby before we drifted apart, the stress it caused with my parents was not good and he wondered several times when he got to my age whether they would split up and the damage it caused to both him and my sister at school was borderline just plain terrible, leaving them both struggling for years afterwards right into their twenties and any adult relationships they both had.

In hindsight, I should have invited at least Bobby at least once or twice after I left Chorlton to come and stop with me in London and everywhere I lived and I regret this, really regret this in hindsight but my life was too unstable, and over those few years after leaving university, every time I spoke to Bobby I guess for a good two years I had either moved address (some of which were my fault), changed partner or moved on from one job to the other.

If you asked Bobby about this, he would admit the stress of me, his older brother barely living above the breadline and often off the grid, he would admit the stress it would have caused with my parents was horrific when I simply stopped coming home for the better part of twenty years.

I, I I should have done better I know with them all with the damage I caused both him and my sister both at Primary, Secondary and right College and into both of their twenties and their choice of jobs and even partners.

I wish I could say I did things much better with them than I did when I moved back to the area when I first started dating Tara again after the launch of my third novel 'Birth' and then ended up marrying her later on but it didn't.

I wish I could say it was two brothers jealous of each other like it could have been between both Richard and Peter and although that could have been true, it always felt like more than what happened between me and Bobby.

I don't want to recap 'Birth' as the story of my band 'Siren' and how I met Tara there, which turned my life inside out there is told there, but the after-effects haunted me for the rest of my life and everybody who knew me I dare say for the next twenty, or even thirty years.

Frank would have been there with Bobby I know, in minutes no matter what that thought of each other.

Bobby I know would have then would have got his wife, Paula down there and I hope all of them would keep it civil at least around Tara and both of the girls if not for me, for what Frank would do if he caught him running his mouth in the Horse and Jockey or the Lloyds after the funeral, but I like to think Paula would have prevented that from happening.

Well, at least I hope she would have prevented that from happening after what happened last time between the pair of them.

I missed it before you asked.

I forgot where I was, probably working or looking after the girls while Tara was out working herself, but I knew where I was when I heard afterwards about what had happened between the pair of them shortly after from Tara.

"Claire popped round before to tell me" She began from the kitchen before I had even begun to take off my coat "Frank laid him out in a matter of seconds, one punch Claire told me"

I looked at her stunned. Bobby was a broad guy, and a good inch or two taller than me and had run several marathons and was lean all things considered, but Frank…

Frank was easily 6 foot 4 or 5 and had been boxing for over twenty years at an amateur level retiring formally the year before and had won I guess 17 out of his 18 or 19 fights if my memory was correct.

"What happened?" I spoke in response to her completely shocked over what she said.

"Football" she looked at me a little stunned for a few seconds before she finally carried on "It was bloody football. Bobby got in Frank's face over United beating City in the Derby after they beat them at Old Trafford".

My family despite being from the borders of the Stretford / Chorlton area which is known for being a Manchester United stronghold were Manchester City fans (which sometimes got me grief at School it has to be said) and I knew Bobby had been there going for years and years with some of his friends but had been always been civil to Frank about football, keeping it to a smile and an occasional wisecrack but never anything nasty which could have led to what I heard happened next.

This bit stunned me as I knew Frank had been a Manchester City fan since the 80s when I think Billy McNeill took over or so when he was a lad but hadn't let it take over his life and like Bobby I know was entitled to his own opinion but fighting, yeah…

I had always been of the case it was only Football and would laugh with everybody either that, but I never took it seriously either way and had before put my arms around Frank after a defeat and the rare occasion when City got something different and then rustled Bobby's hair and said we would do that next time also (which we rarely did of course).

That day, it was something different as Tara told me "Claire told me he came straight at him after Frank laughed at him telling him to bloody grow up".

"Was he drunk?" I answered guessing the answer.

"Frank?"

"No, Bobby".

She nodded, "He had been in Lloyds all afternoon. Paula was at her mum's"

Probably for the best there as I don't think she would have been happy seeing Frank lamp him one I thought quietly to myself.

Frank despite being a few years older than both me and Bobby was in great shape for his age, I guess he had to be in his line of work but he was a big man with barely a lump of fat on his huge well over six-foot shape and was easy going enough not to worry about what everybody may have said about him because he could easily back it up if he wanted.

I wish he had been with me when I died on the Riverbank as he was a great man to have at your back if you run into trouble.

"Bobby should have kept his mouth shut" She paused with a cup of coffee in her hand before carrying on a few moments later "You know, Frank. There is only so far you can push him you know and…"

"Stupid git" I cut in then paused before carrying on "And Frank well…"

"Yeah," She nodded.

"Bobby should have kept his mouth shut and not gone looking for trouble in particular with a man like Frank" I was going to say more but I reached inside the fridge for a can of lager before stopping in shock as if I realized what Tara was going to say next.

"None of the bouncers could stop Frank" She turned away almost in shame.

"Jesus" I swore softly.

"Bobby" Tara turned away in shame almost like she hadn't been there to stop him "He, he started laughing as soon as Frank walked in saying who's the loser in Blue?"

"He was well pissed, wasn't he?"

Tara nodded and then carried on "I think Frank had been working all afternoon from what Claire said and didn't even know what the score and Frank tried laughing it off"

"But Bobby didn't let it go, did he?" I was ashamed.

"No" She blushed "He didn't stop, you know what he is like when he gets going with a few pints under his belt"

I did. We were both completely different when we got drunk. I was a stupid, happy-go-lucky who would sit there with a big, silly smile, pass out quietly in a corner or stagger off home, pass out in bed, and hope neither of the girls would scream too much at me the following morning.

Bobby was a different person altogether, and I knew that before Tara carried on talking about him.

"Claire said, he said some pretty horrible stuff about him and Frank asked him nicely to drop it"

"And he didn't?" I knew exactly what she was going to say next.

"No" She blushed "He even went up to Frank begging him to give him a punch thinking his friends would back him up"

I shivered and answered softly 'Stupid Git'.

"Yeah, and before he knew it, Frank had swung for him" She carried ", ploughing through both of his friends he had bought with him and threw him through the table near the window"

I nodded. Bobby would have egged both of his friends who I didn't know but I wouldn't have wanted to have gone against Frank in that kind of mood knowing exactly what he was like if you pushed him too far.

"Do you want me to carry on?" She paused, almost like for a second she wasn't sure if I wanted to hear what came next.

"No" I cut in "You better tell me the full bloody story not that I want to hear it".

She nodded "Bobby staggered up which really surprised me and somehow ran straight back at Frank in tempter almost like a bull in a China shop only for Frank to turn around and say, "For fuck's sake, stay down, boy" and hit him again when he got up again, hard and he hit a table next door to them where the Jenkins were sat"

I knew the Jenkins well. They were a nice old couple who what two houses down from us and loved both of our little girls as if they were their own grandchildren.

Gordon, the husband of the pair of them Tara carried on telling afterwards was furious and would have probably hit Bobby too despite the fact he was well into his 80s and was on a Zimmer frame if his wife hadn't stopped him and called the Police before anybody could do anything else.

Bobby had done a runner by the Police arrived, made a few notes about what had happened and simply went around to Bobby's house and arrested him the following morning.

He denied it completely of course, saying he wasn't there which the Police simply didn't buy a word off and arrested him, complete with a stinking hangover.

Paula, his wife must have guessed what had happened not that she admitted it to Tara nor me simply stating and from what I understand almost told the Police "First I'd heard off it, even though he stunk of alcohol by the time I got back home"

Bobby got fined for that evening and advised gently by the Police not to behave like that again, which made sure he didn't go in any of the pubs Frank went in for a good few months afterwards.

Wisely.

Frank got charged too, but what helped him was the simple fact that he didn't do a runner and waited for the Police to arrive and simply told them what happened backed by about twenty witnesses who had been sat there in the pub watching what was happening shocked.

They let Frank off somehow, although one of the two Police did suggest to him to calm it down a little going forward.

He also apologised to both Jacksons and also did a few handyman tasks and mowed their garden a few times over the rest of that summer.

Bobby, as far as I am aware, did nothing telling me and Tara on a few occasions he would pop round to the Jacksons and help them out with a few errands over the next two weeks or two.

To this very day, I have doubts whether he remembered much about that night, let alone scaring the shit of the two Jacksons.

After all of that, it went without saying Frank and Bobby never really spoke to each other after that. You could argue they were never close in the first place in part because of their football alliances, but before that if they ever saw each other around Chorlton, they were at least nod.

After that punch-up, they simply ignored each other which was probably the right move.

Bobby avoided the question several times I directly asked him.

"I don't want to talk about it, Andy" He said to me first time I asked him the following week in the Lloyds "Paula is furious with me over it".

I would have been too; truth be told and he changed topics twice the two other times I asked him.

After that, it went without saying, they never really spoke to each other while I was still alive. Bobby was too ashamed of what he had done (although he would never talk about it) to talk about it while Frank...

Frank told me in no uncertain way what he thought about him and what he would do to him next time if they tried that again.

I won't repeat all of it, but I can say he used the word wanker more than several times and mentioned what bones he would break next time.

I told Tara about that, and she shivered like me before adding "Bobby got exactly what he deserved there"

I nodded silently in agreement when Frank concluded with just a slight suggestion that Bobby should be a bit more careful about what he said to people who followed a different football team from him going forward.

Frank had his faults, like me, he was far from perfect in more than a few ways like I am which I'll come on, but he is the sort of guy I would rather have on my side in any kind of fight coming at me with a chair in his hands.

I am glad, it must be said he would have been up in the woods as soon as he found out after making sure Claire was with Tara and the girls.

He would also have both of his sister's two lads, Benjamin and Paul, I seem to recall their names looking for clues about whatever the hell had happened to me up there.

I barely knew Paul on any kind of level, apart from one time we shared a few beers in the Royal Oak waiting for Frank who got stuck on his contract role and ended up being about two hours late.

Benjamin, however, if you got him standing next to Frank, he could have almost passed for his actual son if Frank had any sons with the same cold eagle-eyed stare if you crossed him.

Paul was a Security guard at one of the supermarkets on the outskirts of Withington. Benjamin was a different kettle of fish working as a fraud investigator for one of the Job Centre's.

I first met him if my memory is correct a few weeks after I first came back to Chorlton Cum Hardy to live and I bumped into him in the Bowling Green on the way down to meet Tara at hers while both girls were at school.

"Andy," he said to me coming to the back of me.

I turned around to be greeted by a tall, lanky-looking young man who I had never met before who I knew without introducing himself was one of Frank's nephews.

"Benjamin" He shook my hand.

"You look like your uncle" I smiled.

"Yeah, everybody says that" He smiled back at me "I personally don't see it thou"

We both laughed at that, but I knew something was up before he either carried on speaking,

"I'd watch your step in here" I let him change the tone in his voice without carrying on the conversation.

"Hmm...?" I looked at him puzzled but my attention completely changed into worry.

"Joe's on the other side of the bar"

I hadn't met him before I had to be honest, but I knew all about him as Bobby had warned me about him when it became apparent that something was likely to happen between me and Tara again.

"Frank be here soon" He didn't change his angle "We could have a word with him if you want"

After the Bobby incident, I wasn't sure that was a good move I shook my head making a note to give this pub a miss after this for a bit "Nah, it'll be fine. I've got to get Tara and the girls in a moment anyhow"

Benjamin shrugged his shoulders "He's a wet-nosed little shit anyhow".

This was in complete contrast to what Bobby told me the month before when he rang me up almost out of random when I was still living in Blackpool.

"He's poison, Andy" I remembered him clearly saying "Sheer out and out poison. You don't know him, Andy but he moved into the area a few months after you went to university and Tara, I was told fell for him hook, line and sinker"

"Bit of a charmer?" I paused.

"And the rest" Bobby half laughed "He fancies himself as a ladies' man. Paula told me just before we got together, he made a move on her and several of her friends during one night in the Lloyds"

"And Paula gave him the elbow?"

"Yeah, you know what she is like. She marshalled her friends out of the pub before he could near any of them"

I barely knew Paula then, but even then I could see she would have spotted trouble immediately and gently marshalled her friends out of the pub as quickly as possible.

On the night what I was talking about Frank and his nephew, Frank looked at me stunned a little bit when I walked out of the pub with Benjamin just as he arrived.

"Andy" Frank looked at me then Benjamin.

"Frank" I nudged towards Joe "You and Benjamin may want to go and drink somewhere else this afternoon".

"It's Tara's ex" Benjamin carried on softly "I'm sorry, I didn't know him".

"I'm surprised the manager, Carl" Frank nodded towards Benjamin to carry on walking away "Hasn't thrown him out".

"He probably has" I looked at them both.

"Yeah, I can believe you there" Benjamin finished off me looking back inside the pub.

"He's always like this" Tara carried on the conversation a few hours afterwards once we had picked up both girls from School.

I looked at her surprised.

The Tara I knew when we were teenagers wouldn't have taken shit off anybody upon anybody. I could remember being headstrong enough when we first met and was in our band 'Siren' just before we started dating when some dirty weasel of a guy who was double her age made a very oily move at her.

I always remember saying to Danny at the time "Shouldn't we say something?"

Danny's response was casual, surprisingly casual "Nah, Tara's a tough enough cookie to take care of weasels like him" and then left me standing stunned when she well told what she thought of him within moments.

The Tara I met twenty years later when she began to tell me about Joe was a very different woman to who I had a grew, a woman who had been broken down emotionally and I wouldn't ask then, I could see without asking he had likely given her a good kicking once or twice also.

"I'm surprised nobody hasn't given him a good kicking by now" I looked back towards her in the Kitchen wishing I had known this and told Frank and Benjamin.

She shook her head shaking slightly and I rushed over to her "No, please don't. You wouldn't stand a chance against him"

I don't dare I probably wouldn't have stood much of a chance against him, as he was a good half a foot taller than me at least and probably a good three or four stone heavier than me. That didn't bother me too much, but it was that look in his eyes that worried me and whatever the hell he had done to Tara.

I have no doubt now that I am dead, the Police would have called round on his front door fairly quickly to have a gentle word you could say straight away after Frank had done so first, and while they won't have anything on to arrest him, I would hope they would terrify him enough to hopefully move areas, well away from Tara, the girls and our families.

I should have seen it with Joe, that first time I saw in the pub with Frank and Benjamin and although I didn't really know what he was like, he generally afraid, and Frank said looking out of one of the windows at the Lloyds a few minutes later "Yeah, you are best avoiding him, Andy"

"I am not afraid of him" I stated, and I wasn't.

"I am" Benjamin put his hands around his pint shaking a little "He's not all there".

"I'm not" Frank said.

Benjamin looked at him. He knew what his uncle was like.

I didn't answer straight away, but there was a look in his eyes that showed there was no give in him, there never was and never will be.

I was not like that, and they both knew sat there without answering me.

I am not sure now even now if I really liked him, but he knew he would never hurt Claire or us, and that was good enough for me.

Regarding Joe, we bumped into him, I guess maybe a month later walking round the back of the Precedent slowly back home.

It wasn't even lunchtime and I for a few seconds thought he was drunk before I realised much to my horror, he quite likely wasn't.

"Andy" Tara whispered to me seeing him seconds before I did.

He just stopped, looked at me and spat on the floor before saying "Tara".

She wouldn't look at him directly and simply nodded and simply looked at me "Not seen you before"

"You probably haven't" I half smiled.

"You trying to be clever with me"

"No need to, I can see you are more than clever to talk me".

He looked at me somewhat confused and simply mumbled 'wanker' and staggered off.

I shrugged my shoulders looking away to Tara, whose face was still pointed downwards and carried on walking slowly back home.

Tara would have told the Police about that meeting after I died, and our second meeting which I'll talk about later.

I hope Joe tried running away after Frank and his nephews beat the shit out of him.

I hope the Police ran after him and well…

I hope.

Tara said to me afterwards she generally thought he was going to hit me that day, but for the way I casually treated him by treating it as a half joke and not rising to the bait.

"How did you keep your tempter?" She said to me shortly after he staggered off into the distance.

"With great difficulty" I laughed it off, but my nerves were close to being shot after that, not that I could ever tell her and it took me a good few hours to calm down after that telling her the morning after I had had a late night editing when in reality I was sat there shaking for hours and hours afterwards barely able to move.

I believe Tara first met Joe at the Horse and Jockey, I guess five years after I finally graduated from university and first moved down to London.

Bobby told me about it a few months afterwards and I couldn't say I was surprised.

"He's a total tool" I remember him telling me "Off his head all the time. I know somebody who dated him briefly at college."

"And?" I remember pausing in response to him.

"Well, she lasted six months with him" He paused.

"He beat her" I finished off for him.

"Well," His tone changed "Not just beat her, Andy"

"And?" I was not sure I wanted to hear this.

"Well, he put her in hospital twice, once for getting home late from work half an hour late after she got stuck in traffic".

I didn't envy the poor girl or Tara, but Tara wasn't in my life then, and truth be told I didn't expect to ever speak to her again, let alone start dating her after the

launch of my book 'Birth' and things exploded from there.

I knew she married Joe; she was honest about that almost from the beginning when we started seeing each other almost she was worried that would put me off wanting to date her.

"I wouldn't blame you if you wouldn't want to walk out of that door" She began I always remember not long after Bobby and Paula left after my book launch.

"You've got two daughters by him" I laughed slightly a bit surprised "It's none of my business there why you did or didn't. We are both grown adults; we have both made mistakes. It's only natural".

I found out shortly after, she ended up married to him for 6 years and was living in a very on-off relationship for the next 3 years until I stumbled onto the scene.

"I should have known it wouldn't work right from the off" I remember her telling me in the Lloyds after she had told she was still married to him a few dates in I guess.

"We all make mistakes" I smiled taking her hand "I ran away from here instead of trying to sort things out with you"

"I was a mess then" She looked at me with a sad look "I should have known. You were not my first... "She stumbled on her words.

"It was a long time ago" I smiled "I was very young; we were both very young. I don't think you were ready for a proper relationship, God knows I don't think I was".

We were both young, too young and if she didn't know, I realised it afterwards but by that stage, I was struggling to get by in London and then everywhere that came afterwards.

If you read 'Birth', you may have worked it out that we dated I guess for somewhere around 6 months or so, but knew each other during the time we were in 'Siren' with her brother, Danny I guess for about 18 months of which the story is best repeated there, only for her not sure why she came to watch during my book launch twenty years or so after I originally left.

"I don't know why I went to your book launch" She openly said to me when we met up a few nights later before I returned to Blackpool before concluding with a slight smile "Perhaps it was magic, I was just curious maybe, I just wanted to…"

"You left me a little stunned when you walked through the door" I carried on.

"Your face was a picture that was for sure" She laughed "I spent about two hours trying to tell myself what to do, I honestly thought you would have walked into the back of the shop when you saw me enter and not come back out until I left".

"I could have done that; I think I was too shocked" I smiled.

"I think Bobby and Paula would have beat you up if you had tried that"

I shrugged my shoulders. "I couldn't have got out of that window in the toilet in the back of the shop".

"Yeah, you maybe, certainly not me" She laughed slightly, her shoulders shaking slightly.

Looking back, I guess she must have been as terrified as I was when she walked into that bookshop five minutes before I was due to speak.

The book itself had come out what I guess a week or so before that launch, and the epilogue in the book was written quickly, possibly too quickly after what happened upon a little bit of pushing by my publisher (which caused a delay by about a month and confused a few of the early reviews) so it's possible she may have read the rough proof before the night.

I know Bobby and Paula had seen the proof copies which were of course minus that epilogue so it's not impossible one of them could have passed it over to her to read or simply just told her I was back in town.

I never asked her; some things are best just not being asked.

If you had read 'Birth' you would have left as emotionally drained as I was when the book was finished back at the Lloyds pub across the road from the bookshop.

After the end of the events of 'Birth', I was very in between Blackpool and Manchester for the next few months.

Nothing I have to state was going on between me and Tara at least at that stage.

Looking back at it in hindsight, I think both of us knew it was coming but Tara had her two girls, her two daughters to consider.

I couldn't blame her, there was a lot to consider on both sides, even though there was unfinished business between the pair of us.

In my case, I had just finished with my last girlfriend who was Turkish a few weeks before I came back to Manchester for the reading, Derya only a few weeks before whose father had died a few months before and I think her family thought we might get back together once things calmed down.

Of course, when it became apparent that I was going to get back with Tara, the friction it caused was not great as Derya and I had remained on good terms and she actually came to the wedding, but her family hated me.

I couldn't blame them actually and I was rightly terrified for weeks after the news about Tara and me broke that one or more of her brothers would be waiting around a few of the alleys near Blackpool North train station with baseball bats.

"They hate you" I remember Derya telling me on the day of the wedding "I would avoid Blackpool for a while if I was you"

"I'm sorry" I tried explaining.

"I've moved on" She smiled with a confidence that none of her three brothers had "We were never right together"

"I'm sorry" I repeated myself unsure what else to say.

"It's okay, I understand" She cried slightly "You're in love with her, I think you always have been but they, my family don't see that, they see..." She took my hand and looked at me in a way that went beyond just words.

I knew.

They didn't but I like to think if they had come along to the wedding, they would have seen what Tara and I were like as soon as we probably got back together and then got married, they would have understood.

And perhaps being there for everybody when the news of what happened to me up in the Meadows.

Considering what Tara will be going through now, in some ways I honestly half wish I had stood her up at St Matthew's and not started dating her again eighteen years ago, let alone marrying her two years later considering the misery I know she would be going through now.

It saddens me to think that Jackie, one of her best friends from School met her partner and then later her husband when she was 18 or 19 and he was 21 and got married eighteen months later which makes it crueler for me and Tara that in contrast to them we had barely got going when I died on the pathway towards Jackson's Boat.

I have no idea to be honest whether Jackie would be rushing around to ours when she heard about my death or whether she would sit there at her house in a stunned silence.

I wouldn't hold it against her if she didn't go to the funeral and avoided Tara for the next eighteen months to give her a chance to process what she would be feeling.

When I lived in Chorlton, I remember it happening to one of Jackie's cousins when was in a motorcycle accident and killed in a collision with a Bus and she would barely leave her room for months afterwards.

Baz, I seem to recall his name was a bit of a wild boy at School and got expelled for peddling drugs to everybody behind the bike sheds until he started trying to do it to the teachers too but even, he didn't deserve to get flattened under a 86 bus.

Although Jackie and Tara were friends when we got back together, I was also friends with Jackie although it was fair to say I hadn't seen much of her for some years, that was for sure the way of my life.

It didn't surprise me they were good friends when I bumped into her near the four banks on the way to Wetherspoons a few weeks after we formally started dating and I was finally back in the area.

'Andy' She began after giving me a huge hug 'I haven't seen you in years, what four, what five years'

'Probably six' I smiled back. 'Where was the last time I saw you?'

'Likely one of your friend's terrible BBQs' She laughed 'That friend, Michael was it on Buxton Road. He could never operate that equipment right, could he?'

I nodded my head. Michael of course wasn't his real name, I'll state now that before we carry on as I certainly don't want him hunting me down when he arrives where I am. Michael, I shall call is a great guy who became known for years for doing incredible BBQs with grill after grill lined up all over his back garden so it was almost like a firework display when it finally went dark.

The BBQ Jackie referred there to happened probably a good few years before I died, maybe twenty years, maybe more and I had gone to it with Jackie and her fella Steve, and the girl I was seeing, Ewa at the time during a rare trip up to Manchester.

I met Ewa while in London, and she came up to me twice over the year or so we were together to Manchester on various bits and pieces.

She never met my parents or any of my family.

I forgot the reason why we went up to Michaels, but we were all stunned there within minutes of arriving he nearly set his shed on fire, stoned out of his head.

'I had forgotten he did that' She said to me surprised as the memory came flooding in 'I am surprised we all got out of there alive'

I smiled. 'Let's just say, it was nearly the quickest I had ever been in and out of a party."

Jackie laughed in response and was about to say something else about the party when Tara came up behind the back of both of us surprised saying "I didn't know you knew each other" taking my head gently.

"We went to school" Jackie laughed and then stopped almost like she was realising something before then carrying on barely seconds later "Oh Wow" She paused "I never saw that coming between you two, hand on my heart"

"Thought we would surprise me" Tara smiled back at me.

Neither did I in hindsight looking back at things now after I died and the feeling that has never left me since about Tara like a shiver that has never left my back since I died.

"I thought you would have known" I smiled back at her "Either that or Tara here" I held her hand "wouldn't have been to not tell you".

I wish they were the best of buddies and never argued or anything, but they are only human (we all are) and had a flawed relationship as all of us do, I guess for example when she got together with Steve.

I knew Steve before she met him, and it was kind of my fault they got together for the first time I will be honest. I first met Steve I guess a year after I came back to live in Chorlton when I had to put an advertisement out for somebody to come and replace all the windows in the apartment I had bought right near the meadows.

I knew they were a bloody mess, but I always remember his first words moments after studying them "I don't know what the previous owner has done to them mate but it looks like they have been hanging by a thread of string for years" which reduced the pair of us to a stream of laughter and half a crate of lager before either of it knew it the night after and we became best buddies within days.

Jackie and Steve as a couple, well that was a completely different story when they started dating.

"You're joking," Tara said to me when I told her Steve had been on a date the night before with her "I knew Jackie was on a date last night, but not who, Steve oh my frigging god"

I shrugged my shoulders in disbelief too, it was left stunned too.

Tara couldn't see them together like me.

It wasn't as if they weren't decent people, Steve was 6 foot 3, a quiet, gentle giant who prided himself more in working 50 to 60 hours during the week and then drinking himself into oblivion the following night.

Jackie had her two daughters who were both a little bit younger than both of our girls from her ex-husband who didn't come back from a contract with some engineering firm in Turkey and by all accounts had run off with somebody he met there and although liked a good drink couldn't and wouldn't drink anywhere near what Steve did.

'Poor girl' She laughed after she looked at them both standing at the bar when we went in that afternoon and had our feelings confirmed.

"Poor guy shouldn't that mean" I carried on, my eyes not moving looking at them both.

Tara shrugged her shoulders, "You tell me".

I couldn't answer her, picking out a table for us both to sit on by the door as far away out of eyesight as possible.

"We weren't that much better when we first met were we?" Tara carried on, unclear what to say.

"We were both what 17" I paused for thought.

"Are they both old enough to know better" Tara cut in smiling before I could finish off the thought.

Looking back at it afterwards, I couldn't say it to Tara, but I wondered looking at Steve and Jackie whether we knew what we were doing at 17 and 18, they were both in their early 30s, had their baggage, and had become fairly recently single and divorced/split with children dangling around (even though Steve's didn't live with him and he barely saw them).

Both of their kids were good kids' truth be told, a lot more level-headed at that age than I ever was and I dare say Tara was too as were both of Tara's girls thinking about it.

I wonder if Tara and I would have lasted together for the second time as a couple if I had had children before we got back together as a couple.

I wonder.

I wonder.

I wonder.

'I am glad I'm not dating either of them" I carried on answering Tara smiling at my memories.

"Me too" She smiled back at me.

"I" I looked slowly towards the bar "I loved them both, but"

"They are both still nutters" You carried on laughing in response to me.

'I am not saying that' I looked at her a little surprised 'Steve's a good friend, just...'

'I know' She nodded 'and Jackie's the same...'

Although Jackie and Tara were friends before I returned eventually into her life, they became closer friends shortly after we formally got back together as I did with Steve, almost both of us needed friends outside of direct family and I remember looking back at them worried for some reason or the other I wasn't sure about.

I should have told Tara that I didn't think they were a good match looking back. I think she probably felt the same and was afraid of telling me the same.

I should have seen what was coming next in hindsight between them both, and if I saw it, I know looking back now Tara must have felt the same even if she couldn't tell me then there would be fireworks and not anywhere near the reason we were hoping for then.

I don't know if it would have made any difference to what eventually happened to me like so much else in those last few months, I suspect it wouldn't have if I am honest with myself now, but I simply suspect both simply wanted different things from their lives.

I and Tara were lucky I guess, luckier than a lot of people because we had known each other when we were younger, even though we broke up when we were young, but the crunch point here is Steve and Jackie simply wanted different things from what the other wanted.

I should have seen this coming and that first night I told myself in the toilet they had a good chance of sorting decent happening like it did to me and Tara.

This sadly was far from the truth as it turned out sadly all too quickly.

Jackie didn't want anything serious, while the old saying was Steve wanted something like the complete opposite and pushed it too fast, too soon, way too quickly for either of their sakes whether he would admit it or not looking back.

I remember even suggesting to him gently in the Lloyds to slow it down for his good a few weeks later only for him to turn around and tell me that he would "I'm not going to make the same mistake as I did with Babs (His ex") only for him to then go ahead and make the same mistakes completely as he did with Jackie.

Looking back at over the last few weeks before I died, there was never just one case which directly contributed to my actual death but rather a series of breadcrumbs which built up to an emotional loaf of bread like when during one row Tara accused me of sleeping with her straight after she split with Steve after we saw have a massive argument in the Royal Oak.

Truth be told it had never crossed my mind about sleeping with Jackie.

Hand on my heart, I don't remember what caused the row between the pair of us, but I do remember Tara snapping at me back at home after we had got the girls off to bed. "You're glad they split, aren't you?" She snapped at me before I had even taken off my coat after telling Jackie had just finished it with him.

"No chance" I laughed at her honestly thinking for a few seconds she was joking "Why would I want to do that?

"That doesn't answer my question in the bloody slightest" Tara snapped back at me.

"Don't compare me to your bloody ex" I looked at her stunned.

She turned her back to me and started to cry.

I feel guilty about this I must be honest looking back. I simply shouldn't have said what I said to her and apologised to her there and then instead of trying to get cheap points in a row which I could have defused in seconds. However, instead of simply saying sorry, I was halfway down the road before I knew what I was doing in a fit of tempter.

I had no idea where I was going but was in Wetherspoons around the corner of the Mall in a matter of moments.

"Pint," I said to a bartender I didn't know before then stopping and adding "No cancel that".

"No?" The Bartender looked at me puzzled.

"Yeah" I stopped "Make it a Carling and a double whiskey chaser"

"Bad day?" A voice said from the back of me.

It was Jackie with a large glass of wine in her hand.

"Tara?" She said looking at what the bartender was pouring for me from the other side of the bar.

I nodded and looked at her glass of wine "Steve?"

"Yeah, we've split" She nodded and went back to her seat.

"I heard"

She didn't ask how I knew and instead just changed the topic to simply say "Tara?"

"We've had a row". I didn't need to say anymore.

"I can tell" She smiled "Surprised the pair of us haven't had a few considering your past, and…"

"I'm very patient" I tried shrugging it off "Steve?"

She tried smiling, but wasn't as good at it as I was "I couldn't handle another relationship like he was offering, not after Mike"

Truth be told, I barely knew Mike, but Tara had called him all kinds of names under the sun all of unprinted here but like it had proved with Tara, both women discovered they were both simply best out of it.

Jackie was lucky in the sense of Mike buggered off, where I never found out while Tara well…

I'll come onto that.

"He's a nice guy" She carried on

"Steve?"

"Yeah," She corrected herself "Steve is a nice guy, a really, really nice guy"

"But"? I looked at her.

"I think you know, don't you" She looked downwards

I didn't answer.

"I thought you weren't over Eva when you first back to Chorlton" She carried on.

She was right of course.

"Yeah," I nodded downwards. She was completely right of course.

"I think you know me better than I know myself sometimes" I tried smiling. Unlike my family and a lot of people in Chorlton, they hadn't met Eva, which probably was for the best and looking back, probably explained why I wasn't looking for anybody when I returned to Chorlton to their bookshop to do that reading and Tara walked back into my life.

Jackie didn't answer me for a few seconds and let me sip on my beer.

"We've argued" I paused on my beer.

"You don't say, that's took you over an hour to tell me" Her eyes mocked me and when I didn't answer she looked at me "Over me?" She giggled "Jesus frigging Christ, you rowed over me" and then stopped when other people started looking over at our table.

I nodded bushing and she laughed again and then once she finished laughing I eventually managed to carry on "Yeah, I..."

"Fucking hell" She laughed again "There has never been any tension between us that way. You were hopeless with girls back when you were at school and I never fancied you anyhow, you were like my little brother or something but never more"

"I'm older than you" I corrected her. "Well, three weeks"

"What is age?" She shrugged her shoulders. "It just felt like it then"

I laughed. She was right thou. I was always the dreamer at school, the loner too shy to talk to many people.

"True" I smiled "I was hopeless then"

"Aye not with your writing thou" She sipped on her wine "But girls, don't even we get me started over what you like with girls back then"

'Well, the ones that I wanted to chat to back then" I tried changing topics.

She stopped laughing but her tone teased right across the table '" And was I one of them?'

My answer is perhaps best left across the sands of time, but I was back at the bar and returned with another glass of beer and a large wine for the pair of us.

We both should have gone home after one drink there, not two as it turned out and then three and then stopping out the rest of the bloody night.

An hour later, we ended up having another beer and wine in the Royal Oak, the Lloyds and the n eventually we ended up in the Snooker room in the Lauriston Club heading towards St. Clements Road around the back of the Lloyds.

Although I can play Darts a little if I am sober enough to stand in a straight line, I'm hopeless at Snooker and not much better at Pool before you carry on asking me.

I wish I could say it was down to my rubbish eyesight altogether, but I was always rubbish at Snooker, but not that night.

I am still not the wiser now about how good I played.

"Do you fancy a game, mate?" Some young lad came up to both of us who neither of us knew when we were both at the bar. "Pint to the Winner and stays on the table.

"Andy" Jackie looked at me a little stunned.

I shrugged my shoulders and said "Go on" I followed him to the table.

I had no idea who the lad was, he was maybe 21 or 22 with ginger hair and freckles that covered his face from his nose to both sides of his ears.

"Toss you to break" He flipped a coin.

He broke and potted a red on the break.

I gulped on my drink.

Jackie looked at me like she said I told you so.

She was right as he then popped the black and then carried it on the right cushion to another Red then positioned after scattering the rest of the Reds back to the Black again.

I was going to get murdered I looked at Jackie realising for the first time what the heck I had done.

She looked at me with a look that said I told you so, and I looked at the table. At least it was only a pint I told myself, it could have been much worse.

He then missed the next Red when he spun too much on the White and pocketed both of them much to my surprise and I dare say looking back at it his also.

He went and sat down looking furious with himself, clearly thinking he had completely blown it.

If I had been anywhere near sober, he could have been well right but not with half a dozen pints down as I sliced the white it flew up in the air hit the lamp above the table touching the red when it finally came back now and pocked it.

Jackie whistled softly as if she was saying you, you lucky git, and then whistled again when I pocketed another black after I bounced the white off the pocket around three reds and tapped the black which was then sharply followed by another Red.

The people at the next table stopped playing when they saw that, and then when I sliced the White again and it left the young lad snookered good and proper on the other side of the table, the bar manager whispered to Jackie "Is he doing this on purpose".

It wasn't pretty by any train of thought, but I looked at Jackie sitting down almost as if to say what the hell do I do next?

She didn't know.

I watched him walk towards the table, pause for a few seconds mouth several swear words under his breath, and walk up and down to the other side of the table to see where the reds which were left were bunched together and then walk back to where the white was.

He mouthed another two swear words under his breath and measured his snooker cue across the length of the table.

"Sam" his mate said something to him.

Sam looked at him and positioned it in the middle of the table and I watched the White then smash into the Black which went flying into the middle pocket.

I felt sorry for him.

I really felt sorry for him.

"Sorry mate" I stood up and pocketed the red, then the yellow, then skidded back to the last few reds who were all lined one after the one.

Bang, bang, bang, bn-ang they all went down in perfect order.

I had never played like that before in my life.

He shook my hand and said, "I've never seen anybody play like that before and get away with shots like that"

I didn't answer, leaving it with a simple smile and left it at that.

His mate, Paul, was up next after him.

He was a little younger than him, think they met at Secondary school or something and bought worked for some bricklayer in Stretford I think and he shook my head somewhat more forceful than Sam did, and then muttered under his breath "I don't know how you beat Sam, but you won't do that against me"

I beat him too.

He was a decent player too, but I stumped him on the third Red with a wicked snooker when it looked like he could run away with the game, and then cleaned up after with a good break of 75 and left him sat there muttering under his breath.

"Lucky" He smiled returning with a beer for me.

I was too, but I didn't care. I don't remember about the next lad who came over to me after that, Billy he could have said his name, I think he said was a Butcher and used to play for the kids for Manchester United before his knee buckled during a under-16 match and he nearly played again after that.

I somehow beat him too.

I don't remember the name of the next guy after that but I kept getting free pints every time I won.

After the sixth, Jackie stopped me as drunk as I was feeling "Shouldn't you be going home by now"

I laughed at her, cue in my hand "I'm on a good roll here"

"That's for sure" She agreed "I've never seen you play like this"

I smiled back at her "Maybe after the next game" only to win that game and stagger back to the table to join her when nobody else can forward to face me.

Half an hour later I could barely stand up and Jackie had gone white she told me the following morning and so did the Landlord, Bobby the week after when I bumped into him outside the Lloyds.

"I've never seen you play like that" He laughed at me. "I don't know how you were standing up at the end of it and still winning."

"I dare say you will never again" I blushed. "I am just going to stick to diet cokes after that".

He laughed "And your friend?" He paused slightly for a few seconds.

"Jackie?" I paused.

"I've known her since we were both about twelve"

"That's not what I was talking about".

I knew it wasn't what he was talking about, apart from I spent fifteen minutes kissing her in the toilets and God knows what else.

I didn't even know her name, and Jackie was none the wiser she told me the morning after, when I woke up at hers with about twenty-five missed calls from Tara and about twelve panic-driven voicemails.

I have no idea to this very day whether she rang Jackie or anybody else to this point and I have no idea to this day whom I kissed in the ladies' toilets.

Mags? Paula? Tina? I don't honestly remember.

I also have no idea if anything or not happened between me and Jackie.

I never asked her about it, and I knew the next time I saw her with Steve before they split again a few weeks later what happened or as the case may have happened.

Perhaps it was best in hindsight, I simply kept my mouth shut and how it took three people to carry me out of the Liberal Club into a taxi as I collapsed on the table during my eighth game on the trot.

I won that game too; I was sure of it until I blacked out.

I don't remember, all apart from somebody shouting out "Is he dead?" only for somebody else to then shout out laughing "He's not dead, dead drunk maybe but not dead".

Thinking back, I am amazed nobody called an ambulance for me and have me shipped me off to the local Hospital, but somehow, I believe two or three people got me into a taxi and the taxi took us back to Jackie's.

I am amazed Jackie didn't tell the taxi driver to take me back home, but then again, the state Tara would have been in perhaps a very, very drunk husband unable to stand up would not have been the best move looking back in hindsight.

The reality was Jackie got somehow me back to hers and the first thing I remember was waking up on her sofa with one of her cats rubbing her bum in the middle of my face.

"Thanks" I groaned at her.

"Uncle Andy" I remember the younger one of her children running down the stairs and then started jumping all over the top of me before I had time to blink.

How the hell I didn't swear at him I don't know and instead just stumbled out the words "James".

He laughed and returned for two minutes with Jessica, his younger sister and the pair just sat there looking at me with teasing eyes that reminded me all too well of Jackie.

Thankfully less so of their dad, Marcus.

"Morning sleepy head" Jackie laughed at me from the Kitchen.

She looked rough.

Probably as bad as I did.

I felt terrible.

I felt really, really dreadful.

"I feel terrible" I looked down at the floor.

"I bet you do" She laughed "I don't feel any better".

I tried laughing, only for my hips to start hurting.

"I'm blaming you for last night" She carried on.

"That's right" I carried on trying to be funny but by the time I got to the second word, I realised it wasn't her fault.

It was all my fault.

"Tara's tried ringing me" I looked down at the phone.

"I wouldn't have been surprised if she hadn't" She began pouring two cups of coffee from her kitchen after switching on her Television in the other room for her children.

"Please tell me they weren't here last night" I tried pulling myself up from the sofa softly.

"No" She tried laughing.

"Good" I breathed out.

"Thankfully not, they were stopping at Mum's" She looked into the other room.

I reached over for the Coffee and shivered. I've never really been a fan of Coffee but that morning I needed it, I really needed it.

"Steve's tried ringing me too" She paused a few minutes later when we were both sitting around her coffee table holding our heads "God, I feel terrible, that's the last time I drink alcohol".

"Me too" I didn't know what to say feeling more and more guilty with each second "You are going to see him again?" I changed the topic of conversation again.

"I don't know" She eventually answered, "I mean, he's a nice guy..., God knows he is a nice guy, I don't know, but you two" She held onto the cup for a few seconds "Get back over there, take that from me, it would be a terrible move not getting back over".

I looked around the living room. It was a mess. I had my clothes on, but they stunk, and I am not sure what was off.

I reached for my coat and thought I was going to be sick. I couldn't remember what I had drunk that night but as I got in the taxi, the taxi driver laughed at me "You have a good night last night?"

I couldn't answer him as I sat down in the back of the cab, but the guilt didn't leave me alone for days afterwards.

Tara was worried sick about me when I eventually got home.

"I'm sorry love" I began.

"I know" and hugged back. I simply told her I had drunk way too much, she let it go, and when things calmed down over the next week or so, things went back I could say to a normal pattern.

Well as normal as possible.

I never drank like that again; it took weeks before I would even consider looking at a beer or a glass of wine after that night and I never went back to that club ever again.

I never played Snooker again,

or indeed played Pool also.

Didn't say that some people tried to get me to play off course in particular Markie who Jackie dated after she split from Steve for the second time but that's another story.

I never found out what happened between Jackie and Steve for the second time truth be told the first I heard about it was after work one night when Tara said to me 'Fancy meeting Jackie and her new fella after work tomorrow night?'

I looked at surprised of course 'New Fella?'

Tara turned back to tea in her hands for the two girls 'I thought you knew, they split up the other week, you speak to Steve regularly, don't you?"

I wasn't aware that they had split up again and told her in response to that.

I had ended up bumping into Steve two nights before that while he was working on Hardy Lane. I had popped out at lunchtime to pop to one of the local sandwich shops, and he certainly hadn't told me about the pair of them splitting. Looking back, he had been positive as he always had, and he certainly hadn't mentioned him and Jackie splitting, or he had simply been trying to keep a positive spin on things thinking I had known about him and Jackie splitting.

Truth be told, I hadn't.

I should have seen it to be honest between the pair of them and that had nothing to do with the night at the Snooker Club and what may or may not have happened between me and Jackie, but I should have seen that coming but I have no excuse I missed it completely and without even thinking until now what impact it had eventually towards my death.

Now before I carry on, I don't want you to think Jackie, Steve or the guy she dated next, Marky was directly responsible for my death. None of them were responsible but there is more to this than meets the eye, everything that was a pawn piece on a chess board even if they was not aware of it at the time.

The same also applies to the book launch when Tara came back into my life. I surprised more than quite a few people, including Bobby and Paula when they came along to my reading at Chorlton Book Shop even though they expected it in a little way.

Paula a few weeks after the launch and what happened between me and Tara told me it was apparent that we were going to be a couple again "I should have told you, Tara could have been attending"

"Nah" I smiled, shaking my head "It's okay, it was perhaps for the best you didn't tell me Tara was going to come along, I could have cancelled or..."

Bobby laughed cutting in before I could complete my sentence "I don't believe a word of that, and you know that you would have attended anyhow"

I don't know about that, I tried grinning it off in response, but he was right. Both were right thinking about it even more after finding both Paula and Tara had been friends for a good few years and pleased both of them as did a few other people in the area and my parents before they both died although untrusting to start with saw her for the way she was now rather than the cheating teenager she was then.

"She's done a good job with both of her daughters" Mother said when she came into the Lloyds Hotel with her, the first time they met again with both of her daughters a month or so after I had moved back to the area permanent despite looking terrified every time Father looked at them both.

I nodded in agreement. We had finished badly I knew when both of us were young, but I could see from the first time I saw her with her two daughters, the week after that book launch, she may have been many things both back then and now, but above everything and both of my parents knew above all a good mother.

Mother saw that straight away when she arrived in the Lloyds to meet them both.

I never asked either Mother or Father whether they had seen her around Chorlton after I left for good, they would, they must have seen her around but both of them charmed her in moments when both Mother and Father realised she was bringing up two good, normal kids.

In hindsight, I am amazed Tara's ex didn't do more damage to the kids than he did. I remember Mother asking Tara does they still see them, and breathing a sigh of relief when she looked downwards and said no.

I believed her right from the off there and Mother and Father both seemed to calm down straight after that, and we had a lovely meal and over the next few months, Tara slowly brought them over to see them with me slowly more and more.

I couldn't say Mother and Father were close with her after what happened with us when we were little more than children but I knew they both liked her and loved the two girls.

To be honest, I only met Tara's ex a few times right up to when the day I died, the last time being the day before I died which I'll talk more about in a few moments.

The Police will be knocking on his door after that I know I've stated before and without the risk of repeating myself in a warped way I actually wouldn't mind if they arrested him, but they won't.

I won't forget that Sunday the day before I died of course, as we were over in the Old Precedent when he shouted out to Tara "Slut".

"Andy" She whispered to me.

I nearly said something in response to him, but instead whispered in her ear so the girls couldn't hear what I was saying "Wanker".

She smiled and he started shouting again in Tara's direction "You fat, old haggard slag".

She was a size 8 and was even less than that for the last few years they were together.

"Tara" I looked at her directly, this time not hiding my words.

"He's not worth it" She tried reasoning with me.

"I fucked your mother around the back of Lloyds last night" He carried on shouting. "She was shit too".

Tara's mother had died when she was nine.

Tara looked at me and pleaded with me "No" but I was over there before Tara and the girls could plead with me not to go over there.

"What are you looking at?" He almost spat in my face when I reached him in seconds.

He stunk.

I could smell the sweat all over his body, metres away before I got there.

He had been out all of the previous night clearly; we could smell it on him as soon as he stumbled towards us.

I didn't answer and just smiled at him without saying much.

"She couldn't even give a decent blow job, the old bag" He carried on.

I think he was expecting me to either hit him or just shout something out like "Don't talk to my wife like that".

I didn't which looking back I think surprised both him and probably me looking back at it and by which point when he went on about Tara's mother had gathered a little bit of a crowd leaving him more than a little worried and puzzled at what I was doing to him.

I couldn't blame them.

I didn't have much of a clue either what I was going to do to him, but I knew he had stepped over the line and if I had walked away, the next time we saw him it would be much, much worse.

"Andy" Tara called out. Both girls stood around the back of her terrified.

I didn't answer and didn't move.

I just stood there and watched Charlie start to begin sweating over and over which made me think he hadn't been drinking, rather...

He mumbled something else to which I didn't move and then turned his back and stumbled off swearing under his breath.

I finally spoke when he was 5 yards away, "You aren't worth it" and turned my back and walked back to Tara.

I shouldn't have moved, I should have stood still and waited until he was a good few minutes up the road back to that dirty, run-down flat, he lived in but thinking that was enough turned my back and then missed it when he then came springing back at me and pushed me onto the floor and started kicking my head repeatedly.

In hindsight, I could offer a few reasons why I made the mistake that I made and walked slowly to Tara and the girls none of which make any kind of sense now.

All I can state was the fact he jumped on my back, and I was on the floor in seconds before I could do anything else further and he was kicking at me wildly and I blacked out in seconds unable to defend myself properly.

Where Frank came from, I still even now have no idea.

Perhaps he and Claire were passing by themselves unknown to us too and saw what happened.

I don't know.

Perhaps Frank saw it from a distance and came running full well knowing what was going to happen but either way, Frank pushed him right out of the way and punched him once before I began to start coming round properly.

It was short and one-sided as I got told Charlie stood there looking completely terrified and ran at Frank like a wild bull after a few seconds without saying a word.

I heard Frank say gruffly "No you are not fucking doing that, boy" and grabbed him in a headlock and then threw him on the floor.

Charlie looked at him from the floor and started spitting out blood and started shaking.

Frank hadn't even broken into a slight sweat.

"I thought so" I heard him speak softly "You like dishing it out behind people's backs, everybody knows that. Let's see how dish you it out to me, boy"

Charlie spluttered "Faggot" and tried running off.

He didn't let him get more than a few steps away from anybody and pulled him back. "I've seen your type before" Frank carried on "No, you are not".

He didn't make the same mistake as I did moments before and punched him hard.

Charlie screamed.

Frank didn't give any chance of getting a blow in at him. He punched him twice in the face and then once in the body.

There was no rage from him.

There never was.

That's what I liked about him and was also scared about him in the sense he was always in control and made every blow count when he hit people.

I wish I could say I could have got up and stopped him.

I wish I could have told Frank that was enough to and let him go.

I wish I could have gone up.

I wish.

But I didn't.

I couldn't.

I wish I could have said I simply wasn't in any kind of fit state to stop him.

I wasn't, but I couldn't stop him even if I wanted to.

After the third blow, Charlie pulled himself off and tried hitting him back in a weak manner.

Frank stepped backwards and didn't say a word so his punch missed him completely and Frank just looked at him.

Charlie started to cry.

"Baby" Frank didn't move.

He moved two steps forward towards Frank in a rage the blood and tears pouring down from his face but then stopped almost in a realization he was going to get hit again and then stepped backwards calling out in the distance "I'll call the f&&king police on you"

"Would he?" Claire put her arm to help me stop stumbling as I tried pulling myself up.

Tara shook her head.

"I doubt it" Frank didn't smile. "It was self-defence, not my fault I was trying to protect you and he ran into my fist" He stopped before correcting himself "Fists, it wasn't like what happened between me and your brother, Bobby."

Both girls had started crying and Tara turned to them both "He's gone, he's gone".

"He won't be coming back, well not today" Frank concluded and then turned to look at me "It was self-defense, there are too many witnesses".

The small crowd began to disappear.

Thankfully.

"I've broken into deeper sweats chasing after the Postman" He changed tact "Now let me look at you" He paused looking at me. "I think you're winded, but it wouldn't be a bad idea to get the hospital to check you out to check if that cunt had caused any internal bleeding".

"Frank" Claire looked at the girls.

"Yeah, sorry Tara" He apologised.

He was almost right as it turned out as I had some bruising, but I didn't doubt if he hadn't turned up, I dreaded to think what the little weasel would have done.

I barely knew him, Joe, to be honest, but as soon I started dating Tara for the second time, I knew he was bad news or at least liked to think he was bad news and liked to think he was a hard man until he met somebody, he was generally hard and realised how pathetic he was.

Pre Chorlton, when I used to live in Blackpool before I eventually moved back, I briefly knew a guy like him called Ed who was very like him, and the sad thing is I must be honest Ed, and I were friends for a brief period.

Yeah, Blackpool.

Over time I have forgotten how exactly we met, but I think it would have been something to do when we both signed on at the Job Centre in Blackpool.

It wasn't the first time I had signed on for sure, as that first one they had me in and out so fast I barely had time to blink, but I think the second or third time when he saw me sat there completely emotionally drained.

I've temped in a good few Job Centre's while down in London, and some of them were not the easiest places to work in shall we say, and I generally felt sorry for the poor buggers who worked at that one in Blackpool, I honestly did.

At that point, I was a stranger new to the town and the area who had moved with his partner, fresh from London only the month before only for the relationship to collapse within a few weeks, and for her to bugger off back to

London and the job I had moved down there for to completely collapse also leaving me well the scrap heap as well as completely heartbroken.

How the heck I didn't end up homeless to this death I really have a clue looking back at it, but I ended up in some dreadful little room near the coach station straight after I got my benefits sorted out from the Job Centre and spent about four months there writing and drinking, writing and drinking, writing and drinking.

It would have been the Wetherspoons near the front where I first got talking to Ed, not the Job Centre itself although I dare say he knew my face and he came up after I had just signed on with a pint in my eyes just to settle myself down after signing on even though I couldn't really afford it.

I was close to starting work again with another job, just waiting for them to come back to me with a start date, but I wasn't quite there yet if you know what I mean, so I was cracking on with my 2nd novel, well as much as I possibly could when he wandered up slowly over to me.

"Job Centre?" He stopped looking down at me from the other side of the little table I was writing at.

"Sadly" I smiled slightly back, putting my pen down on the table.

"Fucking Muppets in there, man" He turned away from me and then carried on towards the bar.

I looked down at my pen and picked up my pen again and returned to my pad thinking it was just a random comment, and I would never hear back from him ever again.

Truth to my luck, this was not the case.

I'd barely written a sentence, maybe two more – when I heard his voice come back up to me again "You writing a job application?"

I shook my head smiling slightly "I'm writing a novel"

He shook his head confused.

I smiled and pocked my pen.

"What's one of them?" He sat down opposite me looking directly at the piece of paper I had been writing on.

I honestly thought for a few seconds he was joking and didn't realise until I had put my pen away that he wasn't and couldn't read or write.

DEATH

"It's a long story" I tried leaving it at, missing the irony on myself altogether until after only to then draw more confusion and blank looks from him.

"I don't understand" He carried on.

I didn't know what to say in response to him. I told Tara about him a few years later when I was living back in Chorlton, and I remember her saying to me "How did you get you out of that situation?"

"I didn't know what to say to him"

"No shit" She laughed at me.

"He caught me right out" I tried remembering.

"You were lost for words, now that is something I wasn't expecting to ever hear from you" She laughed at me.

She was right of course, from her point of view, it did sound at best unrealistic he left me completely lost for words, but he did and while we didn't become friends, well not in the sense of maybe what he thought, we became nodding buddies you could say for a month, maybe two or three while I waited for my new job to start.

I next saw him two weeks later in the Job Centre, and he smiled at me from the other side of the Centre before launching into a fistful of swear words at his advisor and then getting thrown out of the Centre.

"He's a charmer" I half smiled at my advisor watching him getting thrown out.

"That's one way of putting it" The advisor's face didn't look up from their computer, but I can tell without them saying anything else, he wasn't well-liked.

I ended up going to the Wetherspoons up the road again afterwards for a quiet beer while I carried on with some urgent edits on my novel I had been asked to complete.

I had just enough savings to qualify for benefits so knew providing I was careful I knew I could survive until my new job kicked in and a quiet beer or two after Job Centre, I knew was perfectly manageable.

"Hey novel man" I heard a voice at the back of me.

I stopped and knew without looking up, it was Ed.

I put my pen down and before I could answer him, he launched into a rather crude monologue of bad language about the people who worked at that Job Centre. I couldn't blame him, truth be told, as they weren't the friendliest of people I had ever across, but they were okay with me.

In Ed's case, they didn't just like him.

As I said, over the next few weeks, I had my savings to fall back while I waited for the new job to kick in and I saw him in there every time after I finished signing on then the pub just after.

Ed?

Yeah, and Ed?

I was never sure, to be honest, and could never tell Tina this for sure but suspected, notice the word suspected he sold drugs on the side if you know what I mean.

Yep, suspected but could never actually prove of course.

Take, for example, his girlfriend Tina.

Well, what I think was his girlfriend. Tina, yeah was

a thin, too thin-looking woman who I suspect was a couple of years younger than him if she wasn't with Ed, I would see her sat on the outskirts of the North Pier most days with a cheap bottle of Cider.

She and Ed had that kind of relationship if you know what I mean when you would seriously wonder how they lasted together when Ed wasn't in the pub with me, he would be outside the North Pier with her sharing her bottle of Cider with him and him his drugs.

It's a horrible thing I know looking back in hindsight how they stayed together when everything I saw them, they did nothing but argue making me wonder whether they were drunk or stoned

Or both.

Ed wasn't too bad when he was with me in the Wetherspoons probably because he drank slower and I made him laugh, but with Tina?

I didn't doubt she had a heart of goal, but when drunk she had a mouth that made me shiver every time, I walked near the pair of them on the edge of the North Pier.

I can't remember the first time I met her through him, maybe the third or fourth time when I saw him in the Wetherspoons a few days after I signed on at the Job Centre again.

I had novel work to do, and I didn't fancy writing in my tiny flat and it was raining outside, and I wasn't in the mood, so I quietly went to the toilet out of sight and sneaked home.

The second time, she shouted out across the road from the Pier a few days later when I was walking past that pier on the way to Blackpool North Train Station "Hey Mister Bookman".

I smiled politely and carried on walking quietly to the train station, not saying anything.

The following week after we signed on, he bought her into the Wetherspoons and grabbed me while I was walking past the back of the pub before I got through the back door.

I wasn't in the mood I have to be honest after having a major disagreement with my agent over the proposed direction of my next novel, but Ed said, "You look like you need a beer, and our Tina is dying to meet you".

I needed a beer after that and told myself I would only stop for one pint of beer, maybe two before going back to face where I was living.

I really wasn't in the mood, but ended up stopping out for three, what four hours and got back to my flat, three-quarters completely drunk.

A week and a half later, they grabbed me outside the Job Centre almost like they were waiting for me just after I got called in for another bloody advisor appointment.

"Come on Mr. Filmman", She lit her cigarette "Ed's told me you're got Brad Pitt lined up for your next film", slurring her words all over the place.

I nearly said I was a novelist and not involved with films so just answered "Brad Pitt" I looked at Ed who just stood there smiling to himself.

"Yeah" He laughed "You said you have his phone number"

Tina whistled and screamed out "I love Brad Pitt".

I nearly said I bloody don't I swore under my breath and was about to say I would see them both around when she grabbed my hand "Come on, you must tell us about what he is like to work with".

"I owe you two beers after the last time we saw you" Ed laughed, and I ended up sitting in there for the rest of the afternoon with them both with her plaguing me with all kinds of questions about Brad Pitt, none of which I answered in the slightest politely avoiding the question.

Four hours in, after she had gone outside for a cigarette, he said to me after talking about how Blackpool FC had deserved the thumping, they had taken over the weekend suddenly changed the tone to say "She likes you, our Tina" almost like it was presenting me a certificate of achievement.

"Good for her" I nodded looking down at my pint of lager feeling beginning to feel very, very uncomfortable.

"She says you can have her for nothing"

I looked at her more than a little surprised and answered completely lost for words "I'll pass"

Tara wouldn't believe me when I told her this story just after we got together instead just teased me endlessly for a good hour or two.

"I wish I had been there to see them" She began.

"No, you don't, I'll have standards you know" I tried laughing it off but then it was a bloody nightmare when I thought he was going to punch me when I turned him down.

"How on Earth did you get away with that?" Tara asked.

"With great difficulty" I reflected remembering Ed when he looked at me disappointed and said "You don't fancy our Tina"

I tried half smiling to calm him down "She's not my type, she's your girlfriend mate, and I don't want to get in your way".

"She doesn't mind" He carried on to me before then, "I don't mind either, I really, really don't mind you...".

I do, I thought to myself and tried to be gentle in response "I can't do it m8, it's not fair on either of you".

I don't remember the exact words he responded with, but it's language that I am not going to be able to repeat here before concluding "I offered it to you man on a plate" and the pair of them stormed off in a huff.

I wish I could say the story concluded there and I never saw either of them again after that, but the reality was this was far from the case.

I should have guessed it wasn't over when he turned up outside my flat at 3 am a little over two and a half weeks later.

I ended up signing off at the Job Centre the week before and started at my new job and ended up staying away from that Wetherspoons pub altogether and even the North Pole thinking that would be enough.

It wasn't enough.

I should have guessed it would never have been enough.

I never found out how he found out where I lived until this very day.

All I remember was buried in my notes when I heard a drunken name from outside my flat start calling out "Andy" over and over.

"What on Earth" I thought to myself and went to my flat window and saw him stood there propping himself against a lamppost.

He was drunk and I saw a carrier bag full of cheap empty cider on the floor right next door to them.

"I thought we were mates" He began as soon as I opened the front door before, I even got to the front gate which likely meant half of the neighbourhood heard his drunken rambles.

I honestly didn't know what to say to him.

He was certainly somebody I would never have regarded as a friend by any stretch of thought. Perhaps somebody you would nod to on occasion and say a kind word, but not somebody you would drink your life away in a pub like he seemed to think we were and after I let him into my flat, I offered him a coffee and apologised simply saying "I've been busy, you know with my new job and err. writing".

"Not even for your old mate, Ed?" He looked at me with pleading eyes shaking his head to my offer of a coffee and instead pulled out a tin of that Cider from his bag.

It only dawned on me afterwards that he'd likely have had a massive row with Tina and likely had found out from somebody in the pub (I don't think anybody in the Job Centre would have told him) and came around to me as he didn't have anybody else to go and see.

Loneliness is a horrible thing I can admit myself and it has haunted me at various times throughout the whole of my life including after I got together with Tara, when she would go to bed not long after the girls, leaving me sitting there looking out across the road from our flat and in hindsight I went down as I was worried about him.

It would be easy to mock Ed in hindsight considering he wasn't particularly an intelligent man by any stretch of thought.

I'll rephrase that on second thoughts, he was intelligent in his way just not the way I would think about it, perhaps closer to the way Tara's ex was in a rat-like, alley-cat kind of way. He I didn't doubt could be kind in his way of thinking for example I would love to have sex with his girlfriend whether she knew about it or not and perhaps pay if I went for the second time or third time.

The reality was to me, it simply wasn't me and simply it would never be something I would ever do.

Unlike what happened with that dreadful beat I took outside Chorlton Mall, which I talked about before, I was polite to Ed.

Well as polite as I could be.

"I've been busy, mate," I said drinking my cup of coffee and watched him drink two more cans of cider in rapid succession in about thirty minutes

"I thought you didn't want to speak to me anymore" He spluttered.

I looked at him a bit surprised and for a few seconds I didn't know what to say to him.

"It's a bit late, mate" I looked at my clock.

It was 1.30 am.

"I've got to be up at 7 am to go to work"

He blushed and looked at his carrier bag.

I felt like an total shit.

"I'll call you when things settle down at the job" I finally found the words not that I believed him personally.

"You promise" He shook my hand almost like he was trying to agree on this by shaking my hand.

"Of course," I said "I'll come and meet you in the Wetherspoons after work when I am a bit more settled in. Just give me a few more weeks" and watched as he left, and I stood there by the door breathing deeply after he had gone for a good fifteen minutes.

I was shattered the morning after work, and the day after that and I have to admit completely forgot about him as the job got busier and busier and I found myself getting caught between a rock and a hard place with my second novel and it.

I simply forgot about him.

I'm not being horrible saying that I just did and the pressure from the publishers over it got to the stage where I nearly threw the bloody manuscript in the Ocean and packed it all in.

Two months later, when it looked like it was finally done, I went down for a walk down to the North Pier late on a Friday evening and stopped outside the Wetherspoons, and then paused about popping in for a drink when I saw him outside one of the bars just off the front which I won't name.

I didn't recognise him, truth be told for a good few seconds, mostly because he had a big grey beard and was wearing a big red shirt but as soon as he opened his mouth, I stood there shocked.

He was in a terrible state too with sick up and down his shirt and two different women, both younger than me by some distance, one blonde, one black-haired on either arm.

I didn't know where Tina was but didn't like the look of any of these women in particular when the blonde one who was probably the older one out of them said "They're not worth it, Ed" looking directly at two bouncers stood outside the bar.

I knew one of them too, not that I would call out to him, remembering him well from the front of the Job Centre vetting people if needed and moonlighting at the bar.

He was a tough nut too I remembered and looked at Ed and thought to myself, Ed for god's sake just walk away if you want to stay in one piece.

I never caught the reason behind the argument between them, but the state Ed was in probably was a good clue and any chance of me jumping in and trying to pull him away from them promptly vanished when he screamed 'Wanker' at them and then pulled himself off his two girls and ran straight at them.

The bouncer laughed at him as he tried blocking both of his drunken punches with ease "Come on, I don't want to hurt you" I remember him saying to him.

I won't repeat the language he threw at the bouncer.

"We can't let you in" The bouncer said "Not in the state you are in"

Ed turned around and started to walk away only for him to turn back sharply and walk back to them furiously, pulling out a knife from inside his jacket.

STOP.

A knife.

I couldn't believe it honestly to God and nearly shouted out 'Knife' to warn them but before he got two yards nearer him, two more bouncers came running out of the club and jumped on top of him with the knife skidding out of his hand within moments.

It wasn't pretty, I would go as far as saying it was bloody nasty as I saw two of them pull him up to his feet and the third of them punch him twice in the stomach and then two sharp blows to his face.

He didn't stand a chance as soon as he pulled out his knife and I saw that even if he got what he wanted which was probably to enter the club. If he got through the bouncers with that knife in his hands, it doesn't bear thinking about it. The Police would have been called, and well who knows what after that.

He should have simply walked away and walked back home and slept it off. The reality was he got his head kicked in instead of trying to impress those two women who were standing there blocked off by the 4th bouncer and looked at each other and simply walked away when they saw him getting his head kicked in.

I carried on walking quietly without saying a word and never went anywhere on that side of town again.

I never heard from him or saw him and Tina again anywhere near the North Pier or indeed anywhere in Blackpool.

Perhaps he or maybe both him and Tina or him and one of those other women moved away to a different town or city, or he spent the rest of his life shitting through tubes in the local hospital.

The thing I learnt from seeing Ed, even if it was as a casual friend, is to know when to walk away to prevent yourself from a friendship or a relationship to prevent yourself from getting seriously hurt in the process.

Tara's ex-Joe was quite a similar man in more than a few ways to Ed and I dare say if I had met him under the right circumstances, we could have been on better terms than what we were, the last time being of course just before I died.

The hostility he showed that day in hindsight I can understand looking back at now probably more than he did. Tara had been his girlfriend, his woman for years and years and he would have hated the fact she had moved on with him, somebody I suspect he would have known about if not from her then somebody else.

Whether we could have been friends or even nodding whatever I was like I was with Ed is open to debate almost right from where we first started talking again straight after I did a book reading at the Chorlton Bookshop then we all decamped to the Lloyds across the road after the reading.

Bobby and Paula without saying anything must have known what was going to happen before we or anybody else did and politely left along with everybody else who had come across with us within an hour or so leaving just me and Tara sat there stunned by what had just happened.

"You were amazing" She began once Bobby and Paula had finally left stunned "I always said you had talent, I'd told Danny this a good three or four times when we were gigging but... "

"Times change" I smiled "I'm not the shy 16, 17-year kid now... "I paused thinking about what we were like for a few moments when were in a band with Danny back when we were all teenagers. "Besides which Danny was the real star; I was just a beginner vocalist"

She laughed in response to that "And I was the eye candy designed to bring in all of the men to watch"

"I didn't say that" I laughed in response.

"Thanks" She blushed.

"Well... "I stopped speaking, I didn't know how to answer her there. I had no more jokes, no wisecracks, nothing else left I could say.

All we had was history.

She put her glass down "Bit like now. "

I shook my head "You were your person in the band, it was as much as your band as much as Danny's. We were all just cogs in a machine that burnt itself out quicker than it possibly should have done".

She nodded "I'm sorry over Eric" repeating what she had told me in the bookshop.

I didn't blame her for her and Eric, our bass player in the band having an affair when we were both in the band.

Eric was ten, twelve years than both of us and had toured all over the Northwest and beyond England and even into Europe with a good few semi-famous bands.

He probably charmed her off her feet.

"I went to his funeral a few years back" She looked downstairs.

I hadn't heard.

"I stayed out of the way" She continued "Danny couldn't make it. I saw Brownie afterwards at the Royal Oak. He looked at me and went to the toilet and didn't come back out until I left.

Brownie was our drummer.

I loved him.

He was a huge, huge Irish man who hit the drums more gently than a man of his size should have ever been able to do so and I heard afterwards tried to get Danny and Tara to make it up afterwards only to realise the gulf between them was massive enough to give up and go back to his jazz bands.

"I went to his funeral too the year before you came back" She looked down and began crying. I put my arm around hers, I didn't know what to do, and before I knew she tried to kiss me before then pulling back to where she was sitting before being shocked, the drink giving her more courage than she had realised.

I wasn't ready. I blushed a little and laughed it off

"I'm sorry" She blushed "I don't know what came over me"

"It's okay" I smiled "Easy mistake to make" and went and got us both two more glasses of Wine and we chatted for another hour or two before I had to leave to go and get my last train back to Blackpool thinking I would never hear from her only for Tara to then ring me up at home (I don't know how she got my phone number to this day – I'm guessing Jackie or maybe Paula and Bobby between the pair of them may have passed my number over to her and we ended up meeting two weeks later when I could get back down to Chorlton in the Lloyds.

She brought both of her daughters down with her not telling either of them about our history and then watched there completely stunned when I started giving them both writing lessons much to Tara's total surprise in the pub.

I was surprised a little when they both asked her what I do workwise and she said I was a writer and one of them, I don't remember which one of them asked if I could show them how to write a story.

"Sure" I reached inside my bag and then ripped out a few pieces from my notepad in my bag and began "You did this" and before anybody knew it in the space of about fifteen minutes, I had the pair of them eating out of my hands.

I found out about her ex a day or two later when Jackie rang me up when I was back in Blackpool after hearing about me and Tara.

"I'd be careful, Andy seriously careful" She began.

"Nothing is going on between the pair of us" I responded.

She laughed at him "Now you know I don't believe a word of what you said there. I know you well enough to know you would be shitting bricks about meeting her whether there would be nothing going on between the pair of us or not".

She was dead right whether I knew that or not and I should have known there would have been problems by the way she looked at me.

We were just friends then and I know I told her that.

"You know about Joe?" She answered me softly.

"Her ex?" I said in response "Tara had mentioned him to us. They split ages and ages back."

"He put her in the hospital twice" Jackie's voice wavered "And threatened her countless other times".

"I didn't know but I kind of expected it"

"He's a total and utter madman. I hope you know what you are stepping into, Andy" Jackie paused. "I know of stories when he broke somebody's nose for looking at him the wrong way in the Royal Oak".

"Ouch," I answered her, thinking to myself I shouldn't go to Manchester again, let alone see her if she had this kind of ex dangling around in the background.

Looking back at things now after I have died, the warning signs of how things led up to my death were there even then and it does make me wonder whether things would have ended up differently.

"He's done time" Jackie carried on "Twice I think both for violence, and if Tara hadn't been so out and out terrified of him, I suspect he would done it several more times of those two times."

"Never heard of him," I paused "Glad I hadn't to be honest"

"Yes, you will remember him" She interrupted me before I could say anything else further "He was in the year above us. He was the one who got expelled from school who went after Smallridge with a gun"

I paused. Oh, shit I thought to myself as I did know him after that.

Greasy little fuckwit I thought to myself which hadn't grown up but I didn't like it and I told Jackie that too and spent the next half an hour standing thereafter we called it quits on the phone head down looking at my fridge thinking what the heck was I walking into with nothing but the screams of seagulls fighting on the roof mirroring what I was thinking to myself.

Tara rang me the following night, then the night after that but I was tied up with novel rewrites and meetings with my agent. I dare say by the time I got back to her close to a week later, I dare say she thought I wasn't interested in her.

To make it up to her and the girls, I got down to the Horse and Jockey a week earlier than they expected and left her completely stunned when I rang her up on Saturday morning and told her I was coming down.

"I could have been busy" She tried saying to me.

"Good job" I guessed otherwise, laughed down the phone.

I will state we were still friends when I went down.

I am not sure what we were when I went back thou.

She hugged me when I arrived and when I asked her "The girls ok?"

She smiled sitting back down to me. "They are at their Aunties"

I should have seen it, and I must be honest, I don't remember what we talked about, we went over to the Royal Oak and ended up at the Curry House near Southern Cemetery.

It pains me now to say I've forgotten the name of it, but when we stepped out of the Royal Oak, both of us were stunned to feel it start to snow.

"Where the hell has that come from?" Tara laughed.

"God knows, it's the middle of March" I looked upwards "It never snows in March".

She looked up cursing once, and then slipped.

I reached to grab her to stop her slipping.

I don't know what came over me.

I honestly don't and kissed me.

She didn't stop me.

I don't remember what we talked else for the rest of the night and truth be told much about the restaurant or that night or much about that night apart from well...

Let's just move on, shall we?

I may well be dead, but I still like some privacy over a few things.

The next morning, she woke up in my arms and swore softly "I'm going to be late picking up the girls"

DEATH

I looked at her surprised and said, "You expected this?"

She pulled away "No, No" blushing.

"Me neither" I started shivering slightly. I didn't know what else to say.

"I don't know what I expected" She corrected herself "Mum said she would look after the girls anyhow, let me have a few drinks".

"And look what happened?" I laughed.

"I don't want you thinking I am like this normally" She blushed guiltily.

"Me neither" I held her in my arms for a few more minutes until it was time for us to get up.

Slipping a few extra quid to the hotel manager to make breakfast for two instead of one wasn't a problem, I think he guessed what had happened and didn't seem to mind truth be told, I got Tara back to her mum's.

I was a good deal later back to Blackpool than I planned, but it wasn't as if I had anything to go back to there.

Things got a bit busy in Blackpool with one thing or the other, and it took another month before I could really start planning to get back to Chorlton for good.

Tara by this point had been up to see me twice, the first time by herself and stopped at my flat (How do you live here I remember being her first words in shock?) and the second time, she bought both of her daughters down with me and I ended up in one of the slot arcades on the South Pier until at least 10 pm way which was well past both of the girls' bedtime.

Just turned 11 pm with the girls fast asleep on blow-up beds I had borrowed from one of the neighbors the night before, she stood outside the flat on the apartment and said quietly to me "Are you sure about this?"

I didn't know what to say in response.

It felt weird.

It was weird.

"Yeah," I looked at her.

"Yeah?" She looked at me puzzled.

I couldn't think of how to answer her, so I just kissed her.

"Yeah," I repeated my answer to her and slowly walked back into the flat leaving her standing there stunned.

Bobby was delighted, of course when I rang him up the evening after they had gone.

"You took your time" He teased me. "Paula was beginning to wonder if anything was going to happen between the pair of you".

"Well," I laughed unsure how to answer him.

He didn't understand. He couldn't understand what had happened to the pair of us back when we were kids.

"Don't forget the wedding invitation" He laughed.

"Don't start, we barely know each other" I tried cutting in only to be teased by laughter from the pair of them in the background.

"It's your fault" I finally carried on a few moments later 'If you hadn't....''

"Don't go blaming me for what you did, you're a grown man. You could have just gone home after the book reading had finished. It's nothing to do with us what happened afterwards, as pleased as we both are of course.

He was right of course.

Righter than both he and Paula realised.

Both of our parents were delighted when I told them I was going to move back but I came close to not coming back right until the night before the removal men came to pick up my all too few belongings and I stood there for a good half a hour stood at the edge of the South Pier just before they arrived asking myself was I was doing the right thing.

I didn't tell them about Tara.

I couldn't tell them.

At least then.

"Are you doing the right thing, Andy?" I asked myself three times walking up and down the outside of the South Pier the night before they came to get what little amount of stuff I had in the flat. I didn't know honestly know. Was I making the right move moving back to Chorlton when I was split the past nineteen years avoiding it as much as possible?

I stood there and listened to the waves crashing slowly against the pier. This was now my home; I tried telling myself.

I looked around, I loved the Pier, I loved living by the coastline but then I stopped, I didn't know.

Truth be told, I didn't know, I didn't know. "You damn fool" I told myself, 'You have nothing here, you never had anything here', but whether Chorlton, whether Tara and her two daughters was the right move for me.

I really, really didn't know. I listened to the waves so more, and when I saw two elderly men start to argue twenty yards from me, I knew it was time to go.

"That could have easily been you and Ed" I chuckled to myself walking slowly back to my flat, well if I knew where he was or for that matter really cared anymore but I was laced in terrible doubts all the way until I was halfway down the motorway.

I could have stayed; I could have told Tara and her girls I had changed. I could have rung Bobby and Paula and told him I couldn't do it.

I could have rung my parents and…

I may not have died.

Perhaps if I had stayed away, what next happened wouldn't have happened near Chorlton Water Park.

Who knows?

I could have perhaps; I could have met somebody else

Who also gave a damn about and who knows perhaps could have had a child, maybe three or four, I don't know and be happy, if in Blackpool, maybe Fleetwood, Cleverley's, Southport or God knows where else on that coastline.

I don't know, looking back at my life, I know I could have constantly gone off in all kinds of different directions instead of coming back to Chorlton and dying the way I did in that frankly dreadful method that I did.

Tara broke my heart when I was 18 when we were both in our band Siren and meeting her all of those years later, you couldn't help but understand why I was so cautious when I saw her, almost frightened when was then taken over by sheer out and out terror when we started dating just before I finally moved back to Chorlton.

For the first few weeks after I moved back, I forced myself to take it carefully and tried to take it as slowly as I really could with all of them.

I don't know how Tara felt, but she must have been the same, thinking about of her daughters as she had to ensure they were protected at all costs, in case it didn't work out between the pair of us.

I think it was at the back of both of our minds that the pair of us could easily mess it up again, so we kept it slow, perhaps too slow in some people's eyes in particular the eyes of Bobby and Paula and certainly Tara's Aunty.

I think the situation was looking back at, we were both completely different people from what we were back when we were young to start with,

I had stumbled into a career of a novelist by chance as much as good luck I have to admit while she carried on with her Tarot card readings and storytelling which her grandmother used to do when I first met her when we were younger.

Joe, well Joe was still on the scene of course as I've said before, although he wasn't living with her and the two girls by then. I think it unraveled when he threatened Jackie when she bumped into Tara and the girls in the middle of the shopping mall.

It was before my time of course, but Jackie told me about in Blackpool just before I moved back to Chorlton for good.

"He broke my nose" I remember her telling me about it "I didn't even see him coming until he punched me"

As I found out afterwards, he was very good at doing things like this but unfortunately unlike me when I had Frank who came to my rescue, the reality was he punched her once hard, told her to stay aware of Tara and forced them back home.

She called the Police straight away, and with two terrified elderly sisters as witnesses told them what happened. The Police went round to see him, probably just to issue a warning Jackie thought and saw the state Tara was in and the two terrified schoolchildren and simply arrested him.

By the time he got out of the Police Station, Tara had had the locks changed. I don't know who suggested it to her, but she was also stopping with her aunt, Melissa.

I dare say he felt he had some kind of power over Tara and the girls, but Melissa was a different kettle of fish. A tough, half-Irish woman in her early 50s, she had had 5 sons by her late ex-husband, 3 of them lived around the corner from her.

I liked her, although was a little scared of her in part because of her sons, all of which was generally hard men, so could well imagine Joe walking right up to her front gate, then seeing either Larry, David or Barry and thinking err and walking right back where he came from.

By the time I came onto the scene, he was living in some pretty run down flat on Edge Lane on the edge of Longford Park on the border of Stretford.

I knew the block when I grew up in Chorlton, and it hadn't got any better than in the years since I moved away from Chorlton.

DEATH

I have no idea how he found out about me and Tara but would have loved to have seen his reaction and would dare to guess he kicked off big style, and even more when he would have found out about them moving in with us 6 months down the line.

I asked Tara about me moving in to ensure not to cause either of the girls any kind of disruption with school etc., but Tara said to me when I asked her "I think the three of us need the change, Andy"

Considering what she had gone through in the years she had gone through with the girls dealing with Joe, I couldn't blame her if I am honest, but I wasn't Joe,

And I think all three of them were glad for that.

It's not my place to say he didn't guess what he deserved off Frank when he jumped me at the edge of the mall, I dare say if Frank had been living in the area at the stage when he jumped Jackie, he would have done the same here straight away.

I would tried the same, I will admit.

I would have tried.

I would have done my best, and probably still got my head smashed in,

I can't share what his point of view would have been towards Frank, apart from probably out-and-out terror, towards me, it would have been a completely different point of view, He may well have remembered me from when we both went to School as the quiet, clever, nervous kid who stole his property.

His woman,

His kids.

I barely knew him including before and after the attack which started the path that led eventually to my death, but talking neutrally, you could tell he didn't deserve his family. He didn't deserve a loving wife like Tara or her daughters.

When I first arrived at the scene, you could see what damage he had done by leaving Tara a shaking, nervous wreck who was terrified to talk to me about anything apart from our memories in Siren until she felt she could begin to trust me at any kind of level.

I feel she was terrified right from the beginning when we started dating for the second time and firmly believe she will be terrified of what will happen next now I have gone.

I can't see Joe trying to muscle his way back to their lives with them.

Of course, he would have been out of their lives for too long to realistically have any chance of this happening, and I don't think either of the girls would let him even if Tara wanted to speak to him again and that is excluding what Frank or either of his nephews will do to him.

I remember Tara telling me the night before they all moved in with me, he had turned up

"He stumbled away throwing all kinds of threats when I told him at the front doorstep," she told me on the telephone. "I thought I was going to have to call the Police"

I'm not sure if the Police would have been able to do much, and in hindsight perhaps we should have moved up to Didsbury or the other side of Stretford Mall.

I couldn't have done it personally to either of the girls generally and didn't want to unsettle either of the girls any more than necessary. They were both bright girls, well above average bright girls at school and later college and decided to stay where we were and pray, hope between the pair of us things would get better about Joe.

Truth be told, I don't recall seeing him that much around Chorlton after Tara and the girls finally moved in with me. Perhaps it was simply down to the fact that he knew he had lost the control he had over Tara and both of their girls and had simply given up.

Thinking about the night in Royal Oak again with Frank and his nephew in hindsight after Frank said he had given up and moved on when he pointed out he wasn't alone.

It was true too.

He was sat there with some slight blonde-haired girl, who couldn't have been much more than 19 or 20 who was close to half as young as he was in contrast to her.

'Dirty git' I always remember Frank looking down at the ground in disgust and then changing his tone when he remembered how Joe was and carrying on "Poor sod, I don't envy her there".

"Me also" I nodded in argument.

"Should we say something?"

I could have gone over there with Frank and who knows what, but it wasn't our responsibility. He would have only turned up with somebody else afterwards.

It's horrible to look at things like this, but he wasn't going to learn, we could have warned off the neighborhood about what he was like, but it wouldn't have any difference

I'd always remember Frank saying to me after he had been the crap out of him after he had jumped me around the mall, he was just a chickenshit who knew he had lost control he had lost but I don't think either of us expected this.

I told Tara the night after and she looked at me completely shocked and started swearing right after we had put both girls off to bed.

"I was the same age as her when I met him" She paused looking outside "The same bloody age"

I didn't need to add anything further to what she said and simply put my arms around her. I wasn't quite what she was so upset looking back, but I let her carry-on crying until the anger had gone and she ended up falling asleep on my shoulder watching some god-awful John Wayne Western film and I ended up carrying her to bed.

I never saw him with the second girl he dated but Bobby did, and I remember him telling me in the Wetherspoons a few weeks before he attacked me in the Mall.

"You sure?" I looked at him surprised.

She was around the same age with short, dark-cropped hair and a little nose ring as both Tara and the other girl.

"Yep, it's her, I saw them in Lloyds the other week when I was in there with... "He didn't mention who. Truth be told, I didn't want to know. The pair of them, him and Paula, hadn't been getting on that well, and I think he simply wanted somebody to talk to that night, but I didn't want to know who he was sleeping with behind her back.

I liked Paula, I did from the first time I met her and felt they could be good for both.

She was over with her parents I seem to recall, and Tara wanted a quiet night in with the girls having a girl's night together watching something or the other which she knew I would have likely completely hated.

I forgot what it was, I have to be honest, and when Bobby rang me up asking did, I fancy meeting up for a drink, I didn't hang around and was waiting for him in about twenty minutes.

Two quick pints of lager, Bobby said over my shoulder "Isn't that..."

"Is it who"? I didn't look backwards.

"Joe" He whispered under his breath.

I didn't turn around and didn't answer only for Bobby to look at me with a look which said he wasn't joking.

"Shall we go to the Royal Oak?" I said calmly.

Bobby shrugged his shoulders as if to say whatever and we finished our pints at a slow to mid-fast pace and I left without going to the toilet. It was him that was for sure and I could hear him mumbling already half pissed in the background.

"He's cruising for a fight," Bobby said as we walked briskly across the road.

"Not with me he isn't" I responded a little annoyed "I'm not going to his excuse for a fight".

Bobby nodded and was looking over his shoulder casually for the next half an hour out of the window after getting two pints.

An hour after when he went back to the bar to get two more pints of lager, he sat down in front of me and giggled slightly

"You aren't going to believe this"

"I'm not going to believe what?" I picked up my pint.

"I think he's on the way here"

"Who?"

"Who do you think?" Bobby's face bent slightly down with a nervous giggle.

"Joe?" I spoke softly.

Bobby nodded,

"You're joking"

"Nope, I wouldn't joke about things like that"

That was open to debate I said to him, then saw Joe slowly stagger into the pub.

"I don't bloody believe it" Bobby laughed softly.

"Drink up," I said quickly.

"Do I have to?" Bobby thought I was joking.

"You don't have a target on your back" I looked down.

I don't know if Bobby ever knew about that fight at the mall later as our relationship had completely changed by then., but then he just looked at me, laughed slightly, looked at Joe and said "Yeah, okay. Let's go to the Spread".

He didn't like the Spread much truth be told, and if I am honest, it wasn't my favorite pub in the world either, but we had just settled in with a pint when the bugger followed us in there also half an hour later.

"I don't bloody believe this" Bobby teased me.

I was starting to get worried, truth be told, so we moved across the road to the Horse and Jockey where thankfully he didn't follow us.

It did leave us both ill at ease for the rest of the night, however that was sure and one or both of us looking out of the window on and off for the rest of the night.

Bobby had only heard half stories about Marcus, mostly in passing from me but when we settled down, he turned around and said, "What a loser".

"Loser isn't the word I would use," I said in response to him.

"I bet" Bobby giggled.

"Yeah," I said, "I could use a few stronger words".

While I could use a few stronger words, in more than a few ways I felt sorry for him I must admit.

I hope my death would force him to grow up a bit if he bumped Tara and the two girls. I know it would be too late for the two girls to have any kind of serious relationship with them, but I would hope he would be respectful to the three of them.

I doubt it, however.

Even after he gave me a good kicking, I know for a fact he'll be out around the Royal Oak or the Horse and Jockey on the following Friday or maybe Saturday again, maybe with the same much younger girl I talked about before.

Maybe not or maybe a different one altogether.

I don't know his background, nor what turned him the way he was, but he wouldn't care what happened to me and probably tell one of his friends "You know that wanker, Tara left me for, well he's dead" and then carry on drinking.

As I said before when me and Tara had that horrific row and I ended up wrecked at Jackie's overnight, I was far from an angel in all the relationships I had throughout my life, but I never had affairs behind my partner's backs.

This doesn't mean I didn't come close. I remember coming close, very close pre-Tara with Eve, a Polish girl I dated when I loved in Blackpool before moving back to Chorlton, however, it must be said.

Eve was a tall, slender girl almost as tall as me blonde-haired girl with blue eyes who I met at the reception desk at a creative agency I ended up working originally for a few weeks to cover for somebody off short-term sick when then went on for close to two years.

She came from the district around the back of Blackpool South train station from a middle-class family. It turned out that when I started, she was temping also when I arrived which I found out on the second day in the Kitchen.

"They don't have much luck around here, are they?" I laughed in the Kitchen when she told me she was also temping.

She shrugged her shoulders "I don't understand you".

"Probably for the best" I carried on pouring my coffee and didn't think any more about it, thinking I would be in and out of there in the next few weeks.

The reality was of course the complete opposite.

She was a fair few years younger than me, fresh out of university if my memory is correct from Lancaster and keen to break into the creative industry.

"Your copy is incredible" I remember her telling me in the pub around the corner from the office the third Friday or so after she started and something like my fourth week at the agency after everybody had gone home.

I shrugged my shoulders slightly; I knew it had been going down with the manager there but didn't think anything further about it, so simply said thanks and concluded with "I'm enjoying it, but it's only a short-term thing you know".

"I've read your first novel, what made you want to come and work for us, you're way too major a writer. "She changed gears leaving me completely stunned for a good few moments after she had finished.

"That was an accidental thing, you know" I reflected remembering the slum I was living in London at that point and the dealer who lived next door to me who the main character in it was based on.

"Shouldn't you be working for some hot shot London agency rather "She looked around where she was sat a little embarrassed "Somewhere around here".

"London isn't all what is it made out to be" I half smiled hoping she wouldn't push me for more details about what my experiences in London were like "Blackpool, by the coastline suits me a lot better than working in the middle of the err... Rat Race".

"Rat Race?" She looked at me puzzled.

I paused thinking how to rephrase myself before adding "Power and Money, etc., you know"

She shook her head.

She didn't understand, I should have seen that in hindsight looking back at things now in particular after we started dating the week after another round of drinks the following Friday.

Well, I'll let you guess for yourself what happened there, and I met her parents two weeks after that.

It was fair to say that they hated me straight from the off I must admit within moments of me coming down to their house for the first time.

"Don't forget, put your suit on" she said to me a few nights before back at my apartment before I met them.

"I don't have a suit" I looked at her a little surprised "I've not had a suit in about ten years".

"Buy one" She laughed.

"I don't have the money" I looked at her.

"I thought you made thousands from your book"

"A one-off payment" I corrected her "I do not know when, or if I am getting another payment from them"

I went out and ended up with money I didn't simply really didn't have, buying a new shirt and a new pair of trousers that didn't suit me, and I think they saw that as soon as I walked through their front door.

"So, you write novels?" Her father, Marc said, He didn't like what he saw from the off I knew before I even had the chance to respond to him.

"Yes", I told him the title of the first two novels.

"Eve showed a copy of the first one" He paused "Little bit too left-wing for my taste if I am honest"

I didn't answer and changed the topic to football, and I struggled for another ten to fifteen minutes about how rubbish Blackpool had been that season until his wife called us in for tea.

"Lovely to meet you, Randy," She said when you came out of the Kitchen with a few plates"

"Andy" I smiled laughing "We've got one of them in the next office. People have got us mixed up a few times. I never knew why as he's about half a foot taller"

I knew seconds later before I lifted my knife and fork up, it was an insult towards me, but I didn't let it bother me and carried on as I normally do.

I don't think Eve's Mother was expecting that kind of answer, but I have always been a quick-minded thinker when I had to, and it left her standing there somewhat stumped that was for sure when she let me in.

Fair to them both, I wouldn't have been surprised if Eve hadn't said all kinds of stuff to both of her parents about me before I arrived and I suspect considering she barely knew me when she asked me to meet them, I suspect most or indeed next to all of it was likely completely incorrect.

I suspect this ruined the relationship from the off as it was an uncomfortable meal, and I knew we were never going to have a good relationship within the space of ten minutes when her father turned around and said to him "When are you planning to set up your own practice?"

I wasn't.

They probably wanted her to meet and fall in love with a Solicitor, somebody who had a steady job and would not be struggling from paycheck to paycheck.

"See you Monday" I remember her smiling as she kissed me on the way out, only for her to then phone in sick and stop returning everybody's calls including mine.

I tried ringing her a few times on both Monday and Tuesday evenings after work only for all three times for it to go to voicemail. I carried on writing not thinking about it as I was buried in rewrites and told myself she would ring me back when she felt better.

She never did and I never saw her in that office again.

As a side note, I saw her around Blackpool Tower about six weeks later with somebody else who had a lot more money than me and also was about five years younger than me.

One of those things, I guess.

I didn't worry about it and carried on with my writing. I should have seen it coming, however, and that bugged me for the next few weeks.

would never have cheated on me, I'm not the sort but she had that kind of look in her eyes which was always wandering.

I saw that in a restaurant around the side of the Tower which has now gone, two nights before I met her parents.

"White or Red?" I asked her when the waiter came around to take our order.

She smiled looking directly at the Waiter "I don't mind, surprise me"

"Rosa" I said going straight down the middle.

The Waiter nodded and carried on and was gone in a few seconds by which point Eve then threw me a dirty look and spat out "You know I hate Rosa".

That was the first of it that me as she certainly hadn't told me that before, so I answered "I didn't, you told me to surprise you"

She didn't say anything in response to that and simply stormed off to the toilet.

I sat there for a few seconds in silence unsure whether to laugh before another voice cut in from the other side of where we were both sat.

"Your wife is a little firecracker, isn't she?"

"She is" I turned around to address a blonde-haired lady who was sitting there somewhat amazed at what had just happened. "And she isn't"

"She is and she isn't?" She looked at me puzzled.

"She is a firecracker and no, we are not married" I recorrected myself. She didn't know what to say I could say in response, so I carried on without really thinking any further about it "We haven't been dating that long"

"Good luck" She smiled at me and then turned away. Her interest was lost.

I turned back. I thought for a second about turning back but saw Eve walking back out of the toilet and smiled back at her and we carried on for the rest of the meal as normal. Well, as normal as that relationship went looking back.

I have regrets it had to be said with what happened with Eve, with each of the other 3 girls I dated one way or the other after I originally split with Tara.

All of them I have to state are or were lovely girls, but as with all relationships, it didn't work out one way or the other.

Look at Bobby for example, as far as I am aware he only ever had one girlfriend whom he met just after leaving school and got married to her.

Whether this will be together by the time they get to 60 is another ball game altogether, but having my heart broken when I was 18 forced me to grow up and look at myself differently and then meeting Tara again many years later was accidental you could say but came at a good time in both of our lives.

Five years earlier, I don't think Tara would have been ready for a renewed relationship with me and I damn well knew I wouldn't have been and the man who dated Eve was quite a different man to the one who met Tara sometime later.

Like I said before, pre and during my times with Tara, I was never an Angel by any stretch of thought when I was alive, I dare say most of the pubs and bars in the center of Chorlton knew exactly what I was like when I was alive, and I dare to say a few were probably glad to hear unofficially, of course, to hear I was no longer on the scene be it to call it a word.

The thing to bear in mind was the fact I was never a bad man, I was a reckless, tactless, be it selfish man, I will be honest and admit but I did my best by everybody I knew and loved, be it people I ran away from when I was 18, and didn't return to for over 15 years, I was never a bad man.

Look at the days when I first started drinking with my now also long-dead friend Dave.

I've talked about Dave in great depth in 'Birth' and how I met him when I was little more than a child and stopped speaking to him only a few months before Siren split.

I've been told I'll probably end up seeing him again soon if I want.

Truth be told, I probably will see him but not yet, but I will ask how we managed to find the money to go out every Friday night and Saturday night and even sometimes on Sunday too if either could get out of bed in time then after wrapping up in the pub on a Saturday. but I never cheated on anybody I was in a relationship with.

Dave, however, was very different from me. In some ways I look back at things we were so different as men, you could be surprised why we could be friends.

Perhaps that was why we were good friends, be it for such a short period. While he was a good man in his way, he slept around a bit with quite a few other women but never had any luck getting what he truly wanted, which was basically what Tara, and I found together: that balance that all too few couples find.

Love, partnership, call it whatever you want.

I had run away from home effectually at the first sign of any kind of trouble, and she then moved on to Marcus eventually who proved to be a control freak and tried to make her, and her children's lives a total nightmare.

When we both got together again, it could have well been the point we were ready to find that connection again we found back when we were originally teenagers.

I would dare say, Joe would have been fuming, returning to my previous point would have been fuming and probably dismissed it as a brief fling.

Whether he liked it or not, the truth soon became apparent that this was not the case as the months turned into years and he would have soon realised it was not a brief fling but rather the beginning of a full-on relationship which led to marriage two years later.

Of course, we would and could have never invited him to the marriage and the fact then the children within two years of me coming into their lives had picked up at School in a pleasing way.

The first six months were difficult. I don't need to lie about that, I will be honest with you with both girls as I do not need to lie to you as it was with Tara also in a different.

Whatever the hell happened between Tara and him (and Tara only told me about half of the story I suspect in hindsight) it destroyed her confidence and something I had to help build back almost from scratch gently helping her realise not all men were total bastards.

Both girls were harder, much, much harder to recover from the emotional and physical damage Joe had undertaken on them, however, in contrast to Tara.

It wasn't either of their faults; they had been bought up to treat mummy like she was a piece of shit, and I walked into low levels of violence against her.

I won't say which one of them, but I full well remember one of them biting Tara on the second day they moved in with me after returning home from work early.

I never found out about what caused her to bite Tara, but I heard Tara's scream as I was letting myself in through the front door, and the tears that greeted me.

I dare say if they had been my direct flesh and blood, I would well done more than I did, but I remember rushing over and taking both girls into the other room to give Tara time to calm down and simply told them it wasn't right what they did until Tara came in to speak to them.

I remember the slamming doors when Tara tried telling them they were all moving with me, and she would tell me on the telephone after they had both gone to bed, I wasn't going to be like Daddy was to them, was I?

It was bloody hard work and left me honestly doubting myself more than on one occasion whether I had made the right move for months until things began to calm down thankfully.

I love children, but not having any of my own caused a steep learning curve here and it wasn't the case that they were bad girls.

They had just been brought up badly, and when I got to them, they both reminded me of the way Tara would have been back when she was their age at maybe 10 or 11.

The Tara I knew at 16 and 17 was a right little firecracker who wouldn't take any kind of shit out of anybody. After being with Joe for several years, she left her by the time she got into her mid-30s, she was a bundle of nerves who left shaking at the most minor of noises.

I didn't expect anything less, in particular when they moved in, every night I returned from work or if I was late in the office working on my novel or in meetings with my agents, I could name at least two occasions off the top of my head when one or both of the girls wouldn't leave me alone as soon as I got home from work or wouldn't go to bed until I got back home no matter how late it was.

It pissed off Tara I know looking back but it was a busy few weeks with writing stuff getting in the way all the way and then the day job too unfortunately and I couldn't tell either of them to listen to their mum and go to bed before I back from home.

It simply wasn't my place like when they bit her, and Tara knew that.

It's a thing looking back at your life I have to say looking back at things after you have died, I honestly wonder whether I should have been stricter with them than I was and tried to be a friend rather than Dad or Father number 2.

Would they have listened?

That is open to debate, I must be honest, and I knew that as soon as I got together with Tara again that would be how I got on with both of her girls after the four of us moved in together.

I was expecting all kinds of problems in reflection, but they were great girls when things settled down, and I could have got into a situation which was a damn sight worse than it ended up being between the four of us.

There was a girl at our schools who Jackie knew a little better than I ever did called Marilyn who gave birth to two girls in three years from fifteen to eighteen I seem to recall it was, only for her partner to get up and bugger off overnight with no notice and I saw what they were like when I returned to the area.

Total nightmares.

Both girls could have easily been like that I know, and I like to think I have made a difference in both of their lives.

It hurts me to know I won't know what shall happen to the three of them of course I am now gone and that upsets me more than anything.

I would have loved to go to one of their weddings if they got married and would have loved to have seen Tara give one or both away.

Grandchildren?

I never got the opportunity for any of it.

I've asked the powers up here if I will ever see any of them again.

They wouldn't tell me.

I was amazed honestly when they told me I would see Dave maybe but Tara and the Girls? The rest of my direct family?

All they told me was to wait.

I don't think they have a bloody clue either truth be told.

I know.

Bloody annoying.

I know.

It's not their fault where I am now, but it's upsetting leaving both girls the way they are and not knowing what will happen next, almost like I was dragged away without being able to see a bit more of the story just as it was starting to really get going.

Of course, I could see Joe in them both a little, both had his mousy, dirty blonde hair and certainly over those first few months his nervous laughter and his temper which thankfully eased over time.

Both girls had, more importantly, Tara's wanderlust when we took them on the meadows not far from where I died, no matter for the first time or the two hundredth, they both loved wandering all around.

Melissa would always ask me 'Altrincham or Didsbury today?" when I would take them both onto Chorlton Meadows almost like they both had a little bet on where I would say we would take them on the rare Saturdays I had off work.

I didn't mind either way and was happier just to enjoy the walk like the first time we all walked as far as close to Altrincham, completely not a clue where we were going and neither of the girls cared less right until I sat down out of breath after walking for close to three hours without a pause and nearly fainted.

Thankfully after the three of them began to settle in, both girls began to surprise both me and Tara in ways neither of us were expecting.

Melissa, the older one of the pair of them by the matter of about half an hour became obsessed with art.

This I kind of expected I must be honest more than what happened with Charlie after I got her interested in writing when I first came into her life.

She had a natural gift for writing, Tara and I both thought straight away within months of them moving in with me, but she started sketching out the characters that cropped up in her stories things began to change.

"She's incredible" I remember Tara saying to me when she showed me a half dozen sketches, she had found in her bedroom when she came to see me in our bedroom/study when I was working at home on a Friday.

"I am impressed" I answered when I looked down at it and wasn't lying either. "They are good, no not just really, really good".

Charlie's attempts at drawing and writing, I felt were even better I must be honest than Melissa's, but she wasn't really interested, which didn't surprise me right from the off and a little more surprisingly into football.

"Football?" I said to Tara when she asked me only a few days after we got Melissa her first set of paints "Really?"

Tara nodded briefly "I know, I wasn't expecting it either, turns out she has been kicking around with the boys every lunchtime for weeks, and kicking the crap out of them in the process by all accounts, and well she's being asked to captain the girl's football team at school".

She was bloody good I could see right from the off too, somebody decided to arrange a five-a-side between the girls and the boys.

God knows what they were thinking looking back at that as some of the lads were almost 3 or 4 inches taller than the girls, and I remember Tara saying to me "I am not sure about this".

I couldn't disagree with her more after looking at some of the lads, but she marched out with the two girls, and I turned round to Tara "I think she's going to kick the crap out of those lads."

She did too and got sent off in the second half for arguing with the Referee when she told the referee they should have been awarded a penalty when one of the other girls got brought down.

"She's not got that from me" I remember Tara telling me stunned as the girl's coach had to escort her slowly off the pitch.

"I don't know about that" I smiled and ducked expecting her to swing at me "Truth be told, I thought it was a Penalty, I think the Referee got it wrong".

I was proud of Charlie then who had one of us constantly going to watch her play each match, She was as good as gold off the pitch, I have to admit, on it, well let's say, some of the tackles she put in made me shiver as an adult man when I saw her fly in with a look in her eyes that made pull away several times in shock.

Melissa was too despite being quieter than Charlie, she quickly grew up to be the more thoughtful out of the two girls, which frequently surprised both of me and Tara with some of her requests.

A couple of months before I died, I came home from work to discover Mrs. Ball, her art teacher at college was sitting there talking to Tara.

I had met her a few times during parents' evenings and that jazz and found her a pleasant enough woman, maybe a few years younger than both me and Tara who also had twin girls in the year below Charlie and Melissa at School.

"Mr. Nicholls" She shook my head shortly after I took off my coat.

"Andy please" I looked directly at Tara feeling like I was missing something here completely.

"It's Melissa" Tara began.

"She's not being fighting, has she?" I reacted worried.

"No, no, no" Tara laughed "We've got one of them already on the football pitch"

Mrs. Ball nearly dropped her cup of coffee in laughter at that. I didn't need to ask had she been seeing Charlie in action on the football pitch and carried on "No, it's about her artwork"

"Her artwork?" I answered puzzled "She's been working hard on it".

"Yes, I know" She paused for a few seconds "It's just some of the best paintings I've ever seen"

"Really?" I didn't know what to say.

"Yes" She paused, "I think she's at the stage where she could benefit from going to sort art classes"

I looked at Tara. Neither of us knew what to say.

Both girls had just turned 16, and Charlie had already had her first boyfriend, a lovely, easy-going lad called Mark who was a history student at Stretford Grammer and turned up unexpectedly with me not knowing asking for permission to start dating Charlie.

"I don't believe it" I remember telling Tara after he had gone "Did you know about this?"

Tara shook her head smiling, which left me wondering for weeks whether she did know about him which I didn't mind as I liked his confidence and hope they last.

I only wish I could see how Melissa would develop too and watch her develop with her life away from her bedroom where she was constantly painting and occasionally writing.

"I know somebody at Stockport Art Gallery who has said they are prepared to let her come along and paint with them next Thursday evening, but" I remember Mrs. Ball saying to me on the last parents' evening I was at.

"But?" I remembered answering puzzled.

"We'll need both of your permissions"

"Of course," I didn't need to look at Tara to ask what she thought there about that.

We couldn't get down the following Thursday owing to a last-minute agent meeting over my novel which left Melissa gutted, and a frantic phone call from Tara, but I took her down the following Thursday to the group.

"Mr. Williams" I shook the head of the gentleman who was running the group and noticed within seconds something was wrong.

Something was wrong.

"Mr. Nicholls" he blushed apologizing after saying hello to Melissa who was standing there excited. "We do have a bit of a problem tonight before we start, you do realise?"

"A problem?" I paused "Sorry, I don't understand…." I didn't

"Yes," He looked down at the floor for a second or two not quite sure what to say to me here before repeating to himself to start with shortly after "Yes, we've had to change the model last night after Maggie the original model had to go and look after her mother, and…"

"And?"

"The replacement is doing it in the nude"

"Ah," I blushed.

"Normally, we wouldn't let children in to paint anyhow, let alone with nude models"

"She's 16," I said "Just"

Although technically she was a woman by UK (England) standards, she was still very, very young.

Probably too young for this.

I felt for her, as I knew I was torn.

"Please, Andy, please" She began. I never liked either of them calling me Dad, Andy please, I began as I got to know them.

"Melissa" I looked at her and then turned my attention to Mr. Williams "Mr. Williams" I spoke softly "She's 16"

He looked at me and then smiled a little relieved "If you can keep quiet at the back, it should be fine"

He was right too.

There was quite a large group there, I guess somewhere around the 17 or 18 painters, I helped her get set up and kept out of the way talking to what I think was the gallery manager, Jackie for the next hour and a half who was watching her amazed.

I was dreadful at painting. I was hopeless at it at School because of my colorblindness.

I tried again when I was in London in my early twenties, but never came close to mastering it and gave up after a few months.

I didn't know what to expect of Melissa here, and I dare say some of the painters standing in front of her were thinking the same.

I was expecting one or two of them to go and complain about why this young girl was there, but their reaction at break time said it all.

"Am I doing, okay?" She asked me at half-time blushing when I got her a cup of coffee.

"You are doing great" I passed her a drink; I could see six other artists from that night standing there around her painting whispering to each other.

They were all stunned, I could see them without approaching them and I honestly thought for a good few seconds, Melissa was going to want to go back home, but I just looked at her with a smile and repeated myself gently.

I couldn't blame her if she wanted to go back home but she didn't and went back to her with a confidence that went well beyond her years.

Watching her, I was proud and surprised when I saw her going back again and carrying on with no fuss. Mrs. Brown was right, I thought to myself when she just stood there with the paintbrush in her hands for a few seconds and it dawned on me she had the makings of a major talent, a seriously major talent if she carried on.

Ten minutes after she and everybody else started again, Peter appeared at the back of me just almost out of nowhere "Mr. Nicholls" He began in a shocked tone.

I turned around "Is, is" I stumbled slightly "Is she doing, okay?"

I don't know if he knew what to say in response for a few moments just watching with me before he eventually said "Yes" He stopped.

"Yes?" I didn't understand.

"I've never seen anything like this in thirty years of painting"

"That good?" I was stunned.

"Yes" He carried on "Yes, yes" and was about to carry on back to his board when I stopped him briefly

"She's surprised both of us too. "

"You're a writer, aren't you? A film director, Maggie said... "

"A writer yes" I stopped. First, I had heard of myself being called a film director, however. "A script writer, a film director not quite..."

He blushed. I got the impression he was as staggered with this as I was, and Tara would have been when I got back later and told her what had happened there that night".

"Neither of us, well her mother and me are any good at painting"

He laughed and I thought for a second was going to pat me on the shoulder instead adding "Whatever you do, keep encouraging her, I've never seen anybody like that at that age do what she is doing there at the moment"

I am pleased to say she did carry on, but that's her story and it saddens me now looking back at my life I won't be there to see what she was going to do next.

I think Peter knew more than I could ever begin to realise with her looking back at it afterwards.

"How did she do?" I remember Tara asking after I got home.

She was shattered and nodded off in the car and was in bed a little more than a few minutes after we got through the front door.

"I don't know" I went to my car and brought in the little canvas she had been working on throughout that evening.

"Was the model, nu" Tara looked at me a little surprised.

"Yes" I nodded "The man who was running it came up to me worried"

"And she was fine over this? were they fine with that?

I nodded still in a little shock "It didn't seem to faze her in the slightest. Not sure I would have recommended the model going into her art class at college thou. Not sure if she would have been as respectful with her classmates sat around her"

Tara laughed. "That's for sure"

"She had about six of them standing around her painting during the break" I reflected "You know I am no expert on this" I looked at the painting on the sofa for a few seconds.

Tara nodded her head "Me neither"

We both just stood there for a few seconds after that just looking at the painting unsure what to say to each other before I finally carried on "They thought she had something, Tara a few of them flat out told me that"

Tara shrugged her shoulders looking down at the canvas "I don't understand art, I don't understand art"

"Me neither" I didn't move from the painting "I was experimenting with poetry not much older than her; you may remember and look what happened to me and who I ended up with"

"Aye, you were" She smiled and went to the kettle stopping there shocked for a few seconds before carrying on "Will they, both of the girls turn out, okay?"

I stepped over without saying anything and held their hand "Yeah, they're good kids, both of them and with me as a stepdad and you as a mum, they couldn't hope for anything better, could they?"

She started crying a little, feeling guilty I dare say for asking me that question and I stood there and simply held her until she had stopped crying.

I was so proud of them both at that point, which makes me feel worse now I am dead.

Who would hold Tara now I was gone when she felt shit?

Who would encourage Melissa to keep on painting and sell art galleries?

Who would encourage Charlie to keep kicking lumps out of her opponents on the football pitch and encourage in her relationship with her boyfriend, Mark if she doubted herself and if I believed what I was hearing about just before I died, in college too if they crossed either one of them?

Who would love the three of them the way I did?

Who would?

I wouldn't blame Tara for simply wanting to move.

I am not sure if I could have carried on living in that house after I died like that. I really wouldn't blame her if she decided she would simply sell up and move the three of them off to Spain.

The girls I guess could go to university over there or college or something, and well it would be a bit warmer, and they could live in semi-luxury in Spain or maybe somewhere else when she saw the size of my estate, I was leaving them.

Whether she would indeed sell up or move is a different matter of course, but it is not impossible for which I couldn't blame she would choose to sell the business and the house and take the two girls off to Spain and live in semi-luxury for the next twenty or thirty years?

DEATH

The little business was doing well, very well just off Beech Road, and while I could never have made a full-time living from it, it more than covered the quiet times in between the books and everything else which happened.

If Tara had wanted, she could have made a nice little bit of money if she had chosen to sell up or left the guys to run it on her behalf (I wouldn't have blamed her honestly if she had decided to do that).

Looking back at it, by the time we had got both girls through university or settled into the next stage of their lives, I likely would have suggested let's sell up or either that took a massive backward step from running it and perhaps hired a manager.

Tara didn't think Charlie had much interest in studying beyond A Levels I remember her telling me several times privately just before I died in contrast to Melissa who she generally thought could easily go on to study a master's at least.

I know we disagreed with this several times as I thought Charlie could do anything she wanted with the drive she had in her right from close to the beginning in contrast to Melissa who was always the quieter, timid one of the three of them.

A number of the teachers on the few parents' evenings I was able to go to say the same.

I remember chatting to one of their teachers on the last parent's evening I went to about that, Mrs. Broadstone who was Head of the girls' year in the last year they were both there.

I had never met her before certainly, she was new to the School I seem to recall Tara saying who I am sure didn't like her very much, but I was interested in her straight by the way she looked at me for a few seconds before starting "You do realise, you have two possible borderline genius as daughters in your household, Mr Nicholls?"

I nearly corrected her but let it go, as she didn't know so instead nodded quietly for a few moments "They both work hard"

She looked at a report in front of her and added "And more Mr. Nicholls?" She paused

"More?" I looked at her puzzled.

"More?" She smiled for the first time which took about ten years off what I thought was roughly her age "Who is responsible for Melissa's rather unusual music taste?"

"That would be me, she's wrecked about three of my records trying to play them".

"I did the same to my parent's record desk" She stopped smiling and left me unsure for a good few seconds of what direction she was leading this conversation "They hated me for doing it but loved the fact I was experimenting with other kinds of music, it shows she is thinking outside of the box".

"Not sure if Tara would agree with you there" I did smile then.

"Do the girls fight much?" She looked at me seriously.

"Not really, they are quite close"

"Were they close growing up?"

"I think so" I paused and looked at Tara. She was never very good with meetings like this "Tara?"

"Yes" She looked downwards "The girl's father, Joseph was not an easy man to live with"

She blushed slightly realising her error from before and changed topics quietly "You can see the difference here, Mrs. Nicholls. Who suggested for Melissa to sing Bon Jovi's Wanted as her audition for the School Choir".

'That'll be Tara' I smiled at Tara when the teacher said only for her to throw a look at me which both knew would result in me getting a ton of earache when I got home (which I did).

When the chance for Melissa to join the School Choir came up, I remember she wanted to audition with 'Dead Moon Rising' by Slayer's Hell only for Tara to shoot her down immediately.

"You'll scare them love" I remember her saying very calmly "If you decide to sing that"

"I didn't know you liked them" I was surprised more than determined to get her to change tracks.

"I think you should sing something a bit more poppy, more norm..."

"I hate that word" Melissa looked directly at me making me realise I should have locked away my records a bit more.

Melissa was good at the School Choir, really good with Bon Jovi even though I knew she wasn't fully convinced by the song but when they asked her to then do Boys II Men or something off the cuff afterwards, she refused with a face which looked the spit of Tara when she threw a paddy at me not them and walked off.

I remember looking at Tara when she did this and whispered smiling "That's probably a step too far for her there".

Tara just threw a look at me which said if I didn't shut up, I would live to regret it.

"If Charlie had been here" She whispered to me "This wouldn't have happened".

I didn't answer that, realising for the first time how similar the girls' music taste followed mine which made me feel a little proud but looking at Tara the rows she would have had with them over their music when I wasn't there, not that I would even tell her that.

It does make me smile looking back at things now that I am dead, as I didn't really mention it at the time. As much as I liked the band, that album was never really my cup of tea in the first place. I would have preferred it if they had played their black album rather than their self-titled album.

If I am honest, that album was never really my cup of tea much but occasionally, very occasionally and please I use the word occasionally a lot like my father when he used to come home from a bad day in the office used to like to disappear into his little study to appear from the world and blast out some Scottish bagpipe music until he began to calm down.

While my father listened to a lot of 50's and 60's rock n roll, folk-pop and Scottish bagpipe, Tara soon discovered after we started dating that my taste in music varied from the early 90's Indie kind of music she had known me for it into something a bit more all over the place.

I dare say she wasn't expecting me to be also into extreme hardcore experimental Jazz, Ambient, French hip-hop, disco, drone metal, post-rock, post-metal, post-punk, even post post post bloody punk etc. than anything she will ever realise. Well, anything but pop anyhow when she starts going through my little hard drive connected to the sound system in my car.

It makes me smile thinking about it, I dare say now after I had died, she'd probably sit there flicking through my vinyl collection, perhaps with the girls, perhaps with Danny trying to work out where I had got some of them.

The stories behind some of them are certainly best left forgotten.

The same would apply also after that moving onto my faded-old Sony Walkman which I would go running on most Sunday mornings.

I used to love that old Walkman which I picked up for a pound off some old car boot sale near Stretford Grammer and the few jazz tapes from that same stall for what 10p just on impulse which was me all over which I wouldn't bother playing during the rest of the week.

Just on that Sunday run.

Looking back now, in more than a few ways I am glad I had the chance to explore music more by myself before we got together really, as it helped us both develop properly before we got together, be it for good or bad, and were able to look at things more objectivity which I think both of the girls will be able to things even though I have died.

We met later again than both of us probably wanted later in life, but while I can't quote Tara directly here, I honestly as you may have guessed in my life, I don't think I was in any kind of fit state to meet earlier.

I remember Tara and I going to two weddings when we were together be it for that second time from couples who had been together for at least fifteen or so years and one of them I always remember her telling me 6 months after when they split "Well I saw that coming".

She was right too, and I told her "I don't know how they stayed together so long".

"Perhaps marriage forced them to take it more seriously as it did with us" She answered. "I always knew Marc was dodgy thou".

"Really?" I looked at her puzzled.

"He was eying up one of the bridesmaids" She looked at me surprised "Didn't you see that?"

Truth be told, I didn't spot it probably because I was at the bar chatting to his brother, Bryan who was in my year at School and I didn't have the heart to tell Tara he had big doubts about the pair of them lasting.

"I'd give it six months," I remember him telling me outside the Royal Oak, cigarette in hand.

"Isn't that a bit harsh?" I looked at him more than a little surprised.

"Not really" He put my hand on my shoulder "He's my brother, I can see things that only brothers can see".

Turns out both he and Tara were right in the fact, that he was sleeping not with one of the three bridesmaids at the wedding but had been having an affair with all three at various points leading up to the Wedding.

One of the bridesmaids would not have surprised me looking back but not certainly all three of them which is what happened.

I've said before, I was not an Angel before and during my marriage to Tara and have said I have got drunk before and made a complete fool out of myself for example with that Jackie, but I never went out of my way to go and cheat on her and I like to think this was a little bit older, no so over-sexed 16 or 17-year-old (I'm not sure if I was ever that thinking about it as soon as I finished writing the above sentence).

I'm glad I must be honest I never cheated on her, although I dare say there could have been opportunities if I had been interested.

Bobby, it hurts me to admit he was certainly not like this with Paula.

I hate talking about this, even though they can't hear me but to understand what happened to me when I died, I must tell you what happened with him.

I love my brother, like I just said Bryan loved and I don't doubt still loves Marc, but families are funny things where in the sense they will forgive each other for things that nobody else would.

Marc was a total sod to his wife, and Bryan knew it but couldn't do anything even if he wanted to.

I had the same situation with both Bobby and Paula right from the start when I came back into Bobby's life and then met Paula.

I stated in 'Birth' I know when I said she was good for him, and I mean that now.

Paula is and was a wonderful girl, who became a wonderful woman, and I fully remember when she walked down the aisle, I honestly to God thought she looked stunning.

The problem was Bobby not her or any of her family but Bobby sadly himself.

It hurts me remembering what he was like the night before the wedding when we were in Lloyds just for a few drinks.

"I am not going to do it" I remember him telling him when I came back up with our third round of drinks "I can't do this, Andy"

"I hope you are joking" I put the two pints of beer down shocked in front of him "She's the best thing that's ever happened to you".

"No, you don't understand" He stopped looking at me and looked down at the floor.

"I don't understand you" I answered "You aren't making any sense here"

He didn't look up, sipped out of his beer and went to the toilet.

Ten minutes passed, then fifteen.

I finished off my pint and gave it another five minutes.

I went to the bartender; Paddy I seem to recall his name and said, "Has our Bobby come past here?"

He shook his head and worried and walked to the toilet.

The window was wide open and there was no sign of Bobby.

I walked around the car park and past the funeral director next door to the pub before returning to the car park, but I couldn't find him.

I rang up Paula's older sister, Jessie worried and she began with a slight cackle "You finished off already? We've barely begun here"

I didn't know what to tell her, so I tried it as simple as possible before answering "Far from it" I began, "It's Bobby, I think he's done a runner"

Jessie paused. I could hear her other sister Paddy on the other side of her, and Paula a little bit further afield from both and God knows who else in the background laughing and joking and she went into the other room and finished and answered a few moments later "He's done what?"

I looked around hoping I would see him so I could tell her I was mistaken sadly.

I wasn't.

"Yeah, I think he's done a runner" I carried on after a few seconds.

"Fuck" She swore, "Do you know where he's gone?"

I paused "I could try their house" I added "I can't think of where else he could have gone".

"We'll keep her occupied here, we've got a stripper due around here soon"

I laughed and said nothing there. It didn't surprise me, knowing Paula's two sisters as they wanted to make sure she went out with a bang.

It made sense for me Bobby to quietly just go out for a few drinks with him.

As for him doing a runner, that was a completely different situation.

I dare say I don't think anybody was expecting that.

I should have seen this coming, even though I hadn't lived in the area for countless years.

I should have seen this coming; things had always seemed that little bit too perfect, that...

Their house was deserted I could see from the distance before I got there.

I stopped when I got to their house and caught my breath for a few seconds. There was no electricity on, I looked through the windows in the living room, there was simply nobody home.

I walked around the back of the house. I did not know what I was going to tell Paula, any of them, then stopped at the back door.

Bobby sat there in a flood of tears "I can't do it, Andy, I can't do it".

I opened the garden chair in front of him slowly. I had no answer to what he wanted to say, and I knew as soon as I sat slowly down.

He loved her, I could see that from the first time I had seen them together but looking at him I could then in the blink of an eye see how trapped he felt.

He simply after leaving School drifted into a warehouse job as a forklift truck, then ended up managing the same firm by the time he got to 25 when he and Paula decided they wanted to get married...

He had a good life, but he hadn't lived the life I had had.

"She's a good woman," He said crying his eyes out "I love her to bits, but"

"But" I repeated to him what he had just said then concluded it "But what?"

"There's somebody else" He looked downwards.

I didn't answer for a few seconds and just softly swore "When did this happen?"

"A few months ago," He paused "It wasn't, you have to understand it wasn't planned"

"I know" I put my arms around him to offer some kind of comfort I wasn't sure I should have been offering.

He and Paula had met when they were both just 17 and so if I understand two weeks after he started at the warehouse.

It was one of those things when I suspected where everybody in both the warehouse and the café suspected what would happen between the pair of them before they did, and eventually showing strength beyond her years, she asked him out setting out her plate.

I wasn't there at the time, but I remember Mum telling me what had happened over the telephone a few months after it had happened, and I dare say she was a little taken aback by what had happened.

I saw a picture of her, not that long after and she was a good-looking, scruffy-looking girl, maybe a little over five foot with curly black hair but with piercing eyes that did not miss a trick.

'Apart from the fact he was cheating' I thought to myself as he carried on crying to himself. I didn't know what to say to him, so I kept quiet and let him continue. Turned out he had met somebody out in the centre of Manchester a few months before while out with his workmates, one of the sisters of one of his fellow workers or something came along unexpectedly and he got chatting to her and well....

It carried on.

"I don't know what to do," he said to me again. "I love Paula; you know I do, but..."

I nodded. He was almost trying to reason to himself what he was going to do.

"I am not going to tell you what you should or shouldn't do" I stood up "But I would make a choice and make it quickly, I know what Mum and Dad think about Paula, it'll break their hearts if you get as far as marrying her only for you to then make up your mind and bugger off with whoever this girl is".

He stopped crying and looked at me stunned. "You are not helping matters"

He stood up.

I wasn't and I knew that, but I didn't know what else to say and all I could say eventually "I barely know Paula and whoever this girl is, Bobby" was all I could say, and he knew it, threw his arms up and walked off in a tempter back where

Like I said, I liked Paula. I always had when I met her a month or so before they were due to get married and a few months before I got going with Tara again.

"I've heard lots about you" I always remember her saying to me that first time I met her in Lloyds with Bobby a week or two after Bobby had written to me to tell me he was going to get married out of the blue and asked whether I would be his best man.

"It's probably mostly lies; well, I hope it's mostly lies" I answered smiling when Bobby went to the bar.

"I doubt it" She smiled "What's not to love about a big brother who is almost as good-looking as him and even more flattering and a famous writer to boot".

I sipped slightly on my pint for a few seconds, and she carried with a completely different tone in her voice "You know he's terrified of you going back to Blackpool and never coming back, you realise?"

I didn't answer her straight away, but she was dead right. This was pre-Tara for the 2nd time, and there was nothing to keep me there.

I had my life in Blackpool, I had my job and... I stopped and knew then she was right, more right about things than I had realised and it was only then I began to see him for more the quiet, thoughtful, shy brother as rather a nervous wreck of a man who was terrified of making the mistakes I made at that age and more.

As I stated before, after the events of the epilogue at the end of 'Birth' (which got added last minute to the publication) came and went, there was only one thing I was going to do and that was come back to live in Chorlton and that was excluding Tara, was come and support my family.

I knew I hadn't been there to watch both my brother and sister grow up; I knew I would do my best to be there for their children.

My relationship with my sister is another story which I'll talk about later, but Bobby and Paula began to display cracks in their relationship within weeks of their marriage, even after Bobby finished with that woman and agreed to start acting like a man.

Things, however, didn't improve on the honeymoon when I heard from one of the bar staff at Lloyds, who we'll call Donny for the sake of this story.

How Donny knew to this day, I had no idea, but I remembered bumping into him when back in Manchester just after I and Tara started talking again.

"I thought you would have heard" He began outside Manchester Piccadilly Train Station "Paula caught him cheating on her last Friday".

I shook my head not mentioning my conversation from outside their house just before the wedding "First I've heard of this, what happened?".

"She had gone to bed not long after they got back from work or something" He began in honestly a blunter way than I would have ever dreamed of saying

"and woke up a few hours later to discover he wasn't sitting in front of the television but had gone out and didn't get back until 4 am or so and I don't know how found out he had spent most of the last few hours with somebody in the carpark at the back of Lloyds and promptly went.. "

"Apeshit" I finished off for him.

If I had been there, I would have given him a proper kick up the backside, but I can't honestly dare to think what that would have done to her confidence, but they survived as a couple.

Somehow.

As I said, I'm glad I never cheated on Tara and am honestly amazed she didn't walk out on him there and then go back to her parents and never spoke to him ever again.

The reality was she stayed, and I dare suspect told him a few home truths to quote Tara.

I thought that would shake him up and they would get back to being a happy couple in the months that followed the wedding, the honeymoon and whatever the hell happened in the car park.

For a short time, it looked like they would too, I never heard talk again of his workmate's sister (I never learnt her name) only for it to happen about two and a half years later.

"Once a cheat, always a cheat" I remember Frank telling the three of us in the Wetherspoons the night after it happened.

"Bloody hell" Tara looked at me shocked.

"I was hoping after the last time he would grow up" Claire carried on. "I couldn't believe honestly, me, Frank and the boys went over to Deckers, you know on the other side of Sale Waterpark"

I nodded. I had never taken Tara or the girls there personally, but I had walked past there on a good few occasions, sometimes on the way to Sale from Chorlton when we had fancied a good walk in the opposite direction from Didsbury. "Had you got there before him?"

"Yes," Claire cut in before Frank "We just fancied going somewhere we hadn't been in before and had just started on our starter when we heard a booking say "Table for Mr. Nicholls, Frank turned around thinking it was you, only to see it was Bobby with some young woman who certainly wasn't Paula".

I whistled under my breath when she said that and just turned around to face Tara.

She didn't know what to say either instead "I thought that story in the car park you told me about was a total one-off"

"Clearly not" I shook my head. I didn't know what to say honestly there and I think both Tara and Claire knew. I thought they were both happy when the reality was....

Well, I didn't want to think about it.

"I know he's your brother, Andy" Claire cut in "but there was always not quite right with him I always felt it".

It is worth noting this was before Bobby tried attacking Frank very drunk and you could argue he lived to completely regret it afterwards.

Tara stood up for him "He's being respectful whenever I've seen him"

Claire nodded and carried on "Yeah, but you know what you say about behind closed doors"

She was dead right of course not that I would admit it then or even now after I was dead.

None of us told Paula anything about what we talked about there, but we all had heard the following day that she had changed the locks and refused to let him in, let alone speak to him.

He ended up stopping with some friend of his on Higher Lane just round the back of the bus station, so I heard before Paula agreed to speak to him a few weeks later and about a month or so, he moved back in with her.

I'm just glad they hadn't had any children as I would dread to think of the consequences there if so with some of the stuff Bobby did.

Thankfully he had settled down somewhat by the time I died, but I was never fully comfortable with him after the above, and I think both Mum and Dad knew that. I would have never kicked off with him, you have to understand in front of him, but I just didn't trust him then after that.

I was lucky with Charlie and Melissa as they both accepted me quickly, but I know of any number of cases where male friends of mine have gone into relationships with children who are not theirs, and well, let's just say it ended quickly and badly.

I don't know whether Bobby and Paula had any children after I died, but if they did, I would hope my death would shake him up, or he cheated again say 6 months after I died and she threw him out for good next time…. I'll leave it with you to decide for yourself what happened next.

I don't want to go back to slagging him off again as he has his life to live whether that is with Paula or indeed with somebody else and I have well… Well, I'll let that second bit lie with you for a few seconds but there are a few things to understand with Bobby and none that nice to admit henceforth why we drifted apart I guess not that long after I moved back to Manchester.

I hate repeating myself over and over here, but his actions I know in hindsight were caused by me running away from where I grew up from my demons, but by the time I returned, the damage had been done to others.

He was a bright, unserious child right up to when I effectively ran away, and by the time I eventually returned around 15 years later, my selfish actions had turned him from a happy-go-lucky child to a nervous, terrified child who I suspect probably spent days frightened I wouldn't respond to his initial letter when he asked me about his wedding.

I couldn't blame him I have to be honest looking back.

Looking at things from the other side of the coin, I know for a fact I would have been me too in his situation after goodness knows how many years gap.

I hadn't seen him leave Primary School or spend five years in Secondary School, pass his exams, go and study his A Levels, or get pissed for the first drunk or meet his first girlfriend.

We had simply grown apart by the time he got back in touch.

Yeah, I missed it, and we ended up growing up before I had the chance to get to know him because I had run away from my past leaving him crippled in all kinds of self-doubt, anxiety and self-hatred.

I heard some terrible stories about what he was like at School after I returned eventually, none of it any good.

I like to think I would have rushed back if I had heard any of it, but I don't know if I would have, I have to be honest.

I don't know if I could come back.

The assault with a plank of the wood was the worse story when he was 11, in his first week at Secondary School when two lads in the 4th year beat him up at lunch and made him pay that protection money for months.

The reason? His brother was in that loser band 'Siren'.

He put up with it terrified too, afraid to tell anybody what had happened until it started to eat him up and one afternoon, he simply didn't turn up and instead went to Longford Park and broke off a branch from a huge tree, waited for the two lads in question near the other side of Longford Park and well...

I couldn't blame him, I have to be honest, and am not sure whether I would have done that, I would like to think I would have gone and told the teachers but he didn't, he simply went and waited for the pair on their way home from school and hit the pair of them so hard, they were in hospital for a week afterwards.

They never bullied him again after that thou and got moved to another School quickly to try and prevent any more violence from either side.

I don't know how Mother and Father were able to put up with what happened when the Police turned up with him. I wasn't there, but they must have known something wasn't right months later in particular when they found weapons under his bed, several knives and at least one air pistol and rifle I am sure they were.

If I had been around (which I regret), I would go and have spoken to those two boys in question and told them what happened, instead of what half-arsed crap they got told from somebody (probably their fathers or older brothers) about how pathetic I was on stage when I found out that Tara was cheating on me.

I don't deny it, it was a dreadful moment but if you ask around, people who remember will tell you we 'Siren' were a decent band and would have got better without a doubt.

We were just as plain unlucky, either that we just weren't ready for it.

I still don't even now regard myself as that much of a vocalist, Tara really could sing however if she was sober and played all kinds of instruments, it was Danny, her brother who was the real star with us and went on tour around the world with all kinds of stars making them all sound a damn sight better than what they were really.

I have no bloody idea how he never made it as a major artist in his own right, but he followed my lead (partly annoyed at Tara I don't doubt) and got the heck out of town from what I understood under a year after I did.

Tara told me afterwards that he met with some folk singer who he knew from Didsbury, and the pair of them got offered a few dates in London, and while down formed a 4 pieced band called 'McDonald' or something.

That band split after a few months, and he met some girl singer who was fronting a Jesus and Mary Chain tribute band, after that band finished they formed another band 'Bennett' and they ended up living in Paris for a bit, Brussels, London, Dublin and at least two more places Tara could never remember.

He next worked with another singer who hit the top forty with his debut two singles, and then seemed to settle down in London for a few months leaving me generally surprised when I found out a few years later, at one point he lived only about two streets away from where I was living at that time.

"I know I can't believe it," I remember him saying when I came back from work one night to find him sitting there one night after work, the first time I had seen him in what fifteen years, the year before I died and I said to him he had barely changed.

I wasn't lying to him either, he had barely changed it had to be said, he was a little greyer like I was, but still Danny I loved a bit I have to admit when I was 17 and 18 completely unlike me who probably looked like what he had always sworn he would never end up like that.

"You're looking great, man," He said in response to me "You look like a proper writer"

"Stressed out and half asleep is probably what you mean rather than what you call a writer" I tried smiling back but was unable to know what to say any more.

Tara and I had been an accident waiting to happen but after the band split up originally, I cut off contact with all of them and ignored repeated calls from him until he must have felt as guilty as I did about the full bloody thing.

Tara told me after she started speaking again, then dating shortly after that they had made it up a few years later after their grandmother had passed away at the funeral.

Any hope of them living near each other was impossible as he was constantly touring with two different acts, and both knew it would likely be a long-distance relationship for quite some time to come.

I don't know when Tara told him I was firstly back in town, then we were an item again, but at that stage, if my memory was correct, he was in America, so likely she wouldn't have been able to tell him straight away even if she wanted.

Personally, if it had been me, I would have been really worried about the full situation, I don't dare say I would have at least been cautious or worried about what the hell any sister of mine was stepping back into there considering the way it had finished off the previous time.

However, it was fair to say Danny was always a different kettle of fish to me and that showed as soon as I walked through the front door that evening.

Tara hadn't told me he was coming right that night, perhaps choosing to keep it a total secret or surprise from me, but then again knowing Danny it was not impossible that he hadn't told her also that he was in town until he turned up on our front doorstep.

Either way, the first I knew about him being there was as soon as I stepped through the front door after another long day and I heard a soft voice from the living room in a soft, drawly tone I knew that all too well "Andy, man".

"Danny" I stuck my head shocked around the side of the living room, my coat still half around my shoulders.

I didn't know what to say considering I didn't even know Tara was speaking to him on any kind of regular basis, let alone know he was coming around that night.

"I, I" I tried speaking and eventually finished off my sentence moments "I wasn't aware you were back in the area".

"Neither was I, Andy Man, neither was I" He smiled slightly, then lit a cigarette in his mouth "I had a day or two off from the tour, and thought I would pop up to see the old town and Tara... "

I paused, still in shock "About Siren" I started unable to say anything else.

"That was 16, 17 years ago" He laughed loudly "We were all little more than children, I've been in better bands, and you were not particularly a great singer anyhow".

"Yeah, that's for sure" I sat down, my nerves settling down.

"You should remember I don't bare grudges" He said after a few seconds "Missie here was the stupid plonker here with Siren, not you, m8."

If that had been me who had said that I don't doubt she may well said something and I thought for a moment Tara was going to say something to that, but he smiled at her in a way that is impossible to put down in words and she shrugged her shoulders and passed him over a can of lager from the Fridge.

"I met that French girl, Holly who you nearly married" She half smiled at him doing a half-serious playful dig back at him which left me thinking that was a story I looked forward to discovering more about in due time.

I looked at them both. This was not a story I was familiar with so added "Please tell more".

"We weren't serious" He smiled back at her

I laughed along blankly not understanding in the slightest what was going on.

"Well, we weren't as serious I dare say as she thought she was" He looked at me changing topics "If I had had my way back then, you two would have been married ten, fifteen years ago after we had toured the world for the second time".

"I would killed you before we go to America" Tara interrupted.

"We weren't that good" I sat next to him in seconds with two cans of lager in my hand "To this day, I don't know how you put up with my terrible attempts at singing and writing"

"I've worked with worse, let's just say," he said sipping into my can. "And people with a damn sight worse attitudes than you had".

"And Holly?"

"Yeah" He looked down at the floor "That wasn't my best move there, Andy"

"Tara" I looked over at her somewhat puzzled for more information.

I looked at them both without saying, I was glad both Charlie and Melissa were in bed after getting the feeling of what was about to be said next.

I kept in the background but Danny, although I hadn't seen him in many, many years I could see he was no longer, the cool, laidback, beer-drinking expect guitarist I had known when I was young.

He had simply grown old.

We all had really.

Life had simply got in the way and kicked us around the block a few times as it always does.

The front door went before I could think of what to say next and I looked at Tara puzzled

"It's Claire" She said "And Frank. I rang her just before you got back"

Frank hadn't met Danny before but squared up in his way looking him up and down slowly before finally concluding "So you're the Rock Star, most damn looking one I've ever seen that being the case"

"Rock Star?" He smiled and shook his hand with a lightness that I think caught Frank out a little "Half arsed lucky chancer more like" which had both girls smiling.

"So, when's the wedding?" Claire as subtle as anything chipped in with a directness that Frank and me look at each other "So when's the wedding?"

"Wedding? I didn't know you were seeing anybody" I looked at all of them shocked almost like I was missing a chapter in one of my novels. "What Wedding?"

Danny paused "I was about to come onto that. I've, err... we've hit a bit of a problem"

Frank looked at him then cut in with a wiseness that surprised me "Off License?"

I was going to say something, but Tara shook her head slightly, well enough to stop me asking any more questions which she didn't know the answer too "Yeah, that sounds like a great idea".

Looking back, seeing Danny like this was a bit of a shock, and Frank, I dare say, felt the same. We also went to Lloyds for a pint or two before eventually calling in the Off License instead of just coming straight back home.

Frank looked at his watch outside the Lloyds "We've given them an hour and a half; I think we've probably given them long enough to sort out whatever the hell they need to talk about".

"He's a good guy" I tried reasoning.

"I don't doubt it" Frank looked at me.

I looked at him surprised almost like I was expecting him to say something else. "Frank," I said a little surprised after a few seconds.

"But he's not just come up for a random social call, don't you think?" He eventually said.

"Yeah, that's a point"

"I think he's okay" Frank nodded returning to his previous point "Nothing like that Bobby of yours I think, I hope".

"Well, he certainly was a different kettle of fish back in the day" I answered standing still outside the off license for a few seconds unsure whether we should go back into mine or not "No, god knows nothing like Bobby".

Frank nodded and by the time the pair of us had got back inside there, Tara and Claire both got the truth out of him in the sense he was going to become a father.

It turned out, while touring over in Paris with his band, he ended up having a brief affair with some French waitresses and found a few months later in Washington after thinking it was it that she had got pregnant from it.

I could read Frank's eyes in seconds, and he said as blunt as you are "What are you going to do about it?"

I kept my mouth quiet and reflected on what I had been like in Blackpool and London myself, this could have easily happened to me, I thought and Bobby after some of the affairs he had been having behind Paula's back.

"I can't marry her" He started sweating slightly "I can't marry her, she's a lovely girl, but I have my career to think about, I've got a tour lined up and down Europe with Sam... "

"Well, that's off" Claire cut in before he could complete his sentence.

"I can't" Danny began again "I can't, I'll get sued for thousands if I cancel now and it's set for four months, which will take her close to when she is due"

"Does she have any family?" Tara changed tone.

Danny shook her head.

"Why don't you move back up here?" I cut in of surprising myself and Frank certainly there and both of the girls looking at me shocked "Couldn't you rent a flat up here for a bit and we'll... "

Tara looked at me stunned, then looked at Claire and then nodded a few seconds later.

"Are you sure?" Claire looked at Tara and then looked at Frank.

Frank grumbled and nodded also, and he said a few seconds after that "Okay" He paused briefly almost like he was going to say something else altogether "Get her up, I'm making no promises, but I'll help get her settled in wherever you end up".

Danny had a flat lined up in about two weeks not that far away from us (Friend of a friend of a friend kind of thing) and she followed about a week later, just after he had got the electricity, and the internet sorted out for them both.

I don't know what I was expecting from her I must be honest looking back, but it was completely different from what we got as she was a quiet little thing and was shaking almost terrified when Danny first brought her through the front door.

The night before she arrived, I remember speaking to both Tara and Claire about this and Claire looked at me "I hope she's okay".

I wasn't going to admit it, but I thought the same and instead just said "She's with Danny, she'll be fine".

Tara looked at me "Danny isn't good with relationships"

"Neither was I?" I laughed kissing her on the head.

As it turned out, Nicole was as nervous as us meeting her. She was an attractive young lady somewhere in her mid-20s with a short black-haired bob which reminded me of the silent film star Louise Brooks and could barely string a word together when she sat down in our home the first time.

"I don't know what to say" She stumbled on her words, her soft French accent slipping through in seconds.

"You don't know us; this could easily be the biggest mistake of your life" I tried being funny.

"Andy" Tara glared at me.

"Yeah, sorry" I looked at Tara. It wasn't one of my best jokes, it had to be said so I wisely shut up and let Tara do the bulk of the talking for the next few moments.

It was obvious within seconds that Tara liked her when she took her into the Kitchen to make her a cup of Coffee and Danny froze before finally adding "I'm terrified, Andy. Honestly, I'm terrified".

"I think Tara likes her" I looked towards to the Kitchen.

"But Claire and Frank" He carried on.

That turned out fine when they came around an hour or two.

Frank was a bit stand-off-ish while he made up his mind as he always did, but Claire was over there in seconds too standing there with the pair of us giggling like they were sisters.

"No, I don't think you have anything to worry about there, Danny" I looked at him.

Frank smiled, not adding anything else to the conversation wisely thinking to himself perhaps silence was the best thing here.

The same also applied to both Charlie and Melissa when they both came out from their Aunties afterwards Charlie wanted her to come and watch play football the following week at School and Melissa without telling her went and drew a pencil sketch of her sitting with Tara without telling her and presented it to her without telling her and said "You're very pretty" leaving her in tears.

"She's had it rough, hasn't she?" I looked at Tara as Tara held her.

Danny didn't move from the kitchen just out of earshot.

He didn't know what to say.

"Very much so, "Tara spoke softly as Claire took her into the other room with Danny and Frank following before eventually carrying on a few seconds later after they had gone "Very much so" She repeated herself "I thought I had it bad being with dickhead, it's nothing compared to what this young lady has gone through"

I must be honest, I never found exactly what had happened to Nicole in her past like Tara hinted to all of us,

If I am truthful, I am not sure I wanted to know to be honest here.

After that initial introduction, Danny carried on with his tour a few days later when he had finished organizing the flat, and Tara invited her over to ours for tea a few days after that.

Nobody would admit it, including me, but the fun would start when the baby came along.

"I would not put Danny down as the father type" Steve said to me in the Horse and Jockey at lunch on the Monday a few days later "I've nothing against him from what I can see, but a father? He is the last person in the world I would put down as a father"

"Yeah," I paused looking down at my pint slowly lost in thought briefly.

It had been far from easy taking on the two girls with Tara, I knew but working part-time at my accountants on Beech Road and my various creative projects I guess could end up with some long, sometimes very long hours but I would always be around in one way or the other, but I was not a touring musician.

I was glad I was not like Danny.

"I'm glad I'm not a musician like Danny, at least not now" I carried on.

He nodded "I remember you guys in Siren. We had to follow you at that bloody festival you split up on".

"I didn't know you were in a band?" I looked at him stunned.

"Nothing like your band" He smiled "We never really went on beyond a few local pubs, and that festival we both played at but when Wendy became pregnant with our first one, I wisely packed in"

I couldn't blame him and told him "I can't blame you m8. I don't think we would have got much further if I am honest"

"You never know" He shrugged his shoulders "At least being a writer, at least you are still being creative"

"In one way or the other, I guess" I smiled.

"You grew up," He said "At least I guess your words, your writing helped you grow up"

"I guess so" I wasn't sure.

"But Danny?"

I nodded in agreement.

"He doesn't want to grow up, does he?" Steve looked down at his pint.

"He said he; he had a big tour he legally couldn't get out of"

"And do you believe him?" "He's not going to try dumping the girl off on you lot, is he?" Steve looked at me worried.

I wasn't sure, truth be told, I wasn't sure. I didn't know what to say, how could I? Danny, when I first met him at 20, 21 would have never dreamed of doing anything like that, but over 15 years later, I was left there thinking to myself, as Steve retreated to the bar to get two more pints in how well did I know him or had he changed over time like me?

Or not as the case was.

Looking back at my life now, it's hard to come to terms with how much I changed from the beginning to the end as all of us had like an epic train journey and knew when to get off and go in a different direction I met Tara again for the second time.

Take for example, when I first went to primary school when I was 5 in the 1970's for example, I became friends with a lad who lived two roads away from where I lived called David.

I don't remember a lot about him looking back now I have to be honest apart from the enormous glasses he wore and the fact he was even more useless at playing football than I was and that said a lot so it was a natural fit we would end up being friends quickly disappearing into the sandpit every lunchtime to disappear into our little worlds.

He got transferred to another school when he was around eight or so and the teachers felt he was better suited to his needs whatever the hell that meant.

I was pretty upset, it had to be said, when I found out but moved on in a different direction eventually a few months before and never really thought about him again.

As an afterthought, I bumped into him a few years later when I was in the middle of Secondary School, arm in arm with what I thought was his girlfriend only to find off mother later that day, it was his carer rather than what I thought was his girlfriend.

"Carer?" I looked at her puzzled.

"I thought you knew" She turned down her television for a few seconds before addressing me further.

"I hadn't".

"I know you knew" She repeated "They found out he was... "She stopped unable to what to tell me.

I went back to my bedroom and spent the next half an hour or so looking out of my bedroom in shock. We were only best friends for a short time and could only think of the way we were back when we were kids, only for us to drift apart so quickly.

I never found out what happened to him after Mother told me about him, I heard rumours as you do, none of them good, but I never saw him again.

Looking back at things, Danny was similar, and I guess in a way David was.

I knew him briefly, say for 18 months or so back when I was little more than a child and was like an older brother whom I looked up to who was perfect, had all of the girls after him and was the best guitarist I had ever seen.

My brief time in our band Siren opened my eyes to a different world before I went off on a different journey and kept drifting until I eventually Tara and when I met Danny again in the second half of my life.

"He's not grown up, has he?" Steve cut through my thoughts in the pub.

"No" I shook my head "He's still a decent guy" I paused and nearly said something else altogether "No, he's not changed"

"I know, but is he father material?" Steve laid out the truth right in front of me. "That's the crux question isn't Andy?"

I didn't answer for a few seconds, but Steve knew what my answer was going to be without me answering "No he's not" I said eventually. "You are right"

Steve was right, he wasn't and that is what concerned me and Frank also, who saw it coming out quicker than I did. Tara and to a lesser degree, Claire, both knew it also but couldn't say also, they were also worried he was going to do a runner not long after she gave birth or simply bugger off with some other girl he picked up on tour.

I'll let you guess for yourself what he did, and it wasn't the happy family that his daughter deserved.

We should have seen that coming right from the start, but we all hoped this would shake him up.

It didn't.

He rang her up constantly over the first two weeks on tour almost every night, running up a huge phone bill in the process and then it moved onto Skype and surprised all of us by coming home when the band had a few nights after playing in Newcastle and before the band were due to then go and play in Belfast.

Tara looked at me stunned when he turned up at ours with presents, he had bought both Charlie and Melissa from Harrods in London the week before.

"You shouldn't have done this" She looked at him stunned when he turned up with Nicole beaming at our front step.

He generally looked happy.

"It's the least I could give for my favorite sister" He carried on looking over my shoulder worried that there was nobody else in our house.

"I am not telling Claire that" I quipped which drew a laugh from everybody, but I generally didn't know what to say in response to what he said so simply stepped backwards.

He wasn't my brother, but I was happy for him, Tara and both Charlie and Melissa.

Neither Charlie nor Melissa would leave him alone over that night even when Melissa said, "Uncle Danny, I don't like football" and Charlie quipped "I hate painting".

It was funny watching the two girls stand there in surprise who worked it out between themselves he had simply got it mixed up and dealt with as two adults, which brought back a lot of memories of the way Bobby and my sister were back in the day towards our father when-ever we were away with work, but I didn't know...

And Tara knew I felt it afterwards.

"Too good?" She said to me moments after they went.

"Yeah, sorry love, that was too good to be true" I finished off for her.

"Me too, Andy, I hope you are wrong" She kissed me on the cheek nodding and carried on putting the girls to bed.

I simply stood there by the window, looking outside at the rain.

I knew what he was going to do and felt powerless.

I should said something now looking back in reflection, Danny would bottle it and do a runner within a few months.

I remember my mother asking me something if I was sure about us when Tara and I got back together, she was concerned had we had thought this through when we got back together, only to then be totally surprised when I told her I was never more determined to make it work than anything else in my life.

Danny, it hurts me to admit it now afterwards, I don't know if there was something I just couldn't put my finger on that wasn't right from the first time I met him and Nicole.

It wasn't her like it was his fault in hindsight, as she was generally a nice girl, and he was still the Danny I grew up in awe as a teenager, but the relationship wasn't right for him, and I think we all knew that in hindsight.

I think Tara was hoping this would first result in Danny coming back to live near us and secondly, once things began to unravel between the pair of them quickly, Danny would soon realise the error of his ways and would come back here with her before it was too late.

The reality was I honestly think both he and Tara and I dare say Nicole knew what was going to happen right from when they moved up here.

DEATH

I saw it coming deep down when I was standing outside the Lloyds with Frank on the way back before we went to the off-license and finally home.

Frank didn't trust Danny almost from the start when he first met him when he first turned up at yours. He didn't dislike him, like a lot of other people, but he didn't trust him in the slightest.

The problem with Danny is the fact it was stuck in my head the way he used to be back when we were both little more than children in Siren, our band.

In Siren, he was a borderline genius on guitar and with his very own songs which I heard the beginnings of in rehearsals and a lovely, lovely guy who I think if I am honest, I was a little in love with too.

The difference was, however, although I loved him as Tara did, was he father material?

It was a very different situation to what Joe, Tara's ex was like with their children. Joe of course as I stated before really didn't deserve fatherhood on any level, and while I am not going to start stating I am any kind of saint, I gave both Charlie and Melissa some kind of hope growing up.

Some men and indeed women which hurts me to admit simply are not good choices to be parents and Danny sadly was one of these whether he liked to admit it or not.

When I first met him when I was 16, I should have seen him becoming a full-time musician, and this showed in Siren when he started to book gigs for us all the time.

Some of them were total disasters, it had to be said, and both Danny and Tara and the other guys, if they were still here to say anything would agree, but he learned from that and his next few groups from what I understand, he became very good at that which set the scene for him as a travelling musician.

I saw it back when I first met him when I was 16 and it was what stopped me from asking to do some jamming when he came back into both of my and Tara's lives just before I died, and I could see how little he had changed as a person when in reality, Nicole getting pregnant should have shook him into moving on with his life.

It didn't, however sadly.

I would dare say when he came back into our lives, if me and Tara didn't have the girls to deal with, he would have had us both with a new rhythm section up somewhere up in Chorlton, and if it had gone down somewhere, God knows what else he would have done.

The problem was, I wasn't the man I was then back when I was in Siren with him and Tara. I hadn't even looked at a guitar or consciously written any lyrics which could have half-passed for songs in close to 17 years.

Tara was the same, rushing around constantly after both girls when they weren't in School and as far as I was aware hadn't picked up any kind of instrument since she gave birth, not that would have stopped Danny the first chance he could if we had provided any kind of encouragement.

If we didn't have the girls, or they were a few years than what they were, I don't know, I don't know I have to be honest, we could have been tempted, possibly with the right backing and had some fun, but it wouldn't have be like the way they were, and I wasn't the man anymore I was originally back then,

And Tara wasn't the wild, hippy chick she was back then.

We both still loved him, but we simply weren't the same people we were back then, which is probably why after that evening when he turned up with all of those presents, we simply heard less and less from him and then afterwards Nicole.

We never heard for example formally that they had split right up to when I died, but after Frank said he saw them arguing outside the Horse and Jockey, it was obvious when Tara tried ringing him worried and he only returned her call what about three days afterwards.

I can't remember when Nicole stopped coming around, maybe a month, maybe two after they came around that time.

Tara I know as did Claire tried keeping in touch with him, but he was distant, always on tour or sorting out stuff apparently for him and Nicole in their house, and I simply forgot about them not that I would ever admit to that Tara and Claire and the girls right up to just before I died, I simply forgot about them right up to when I took that horrific beating from Marcus the night before I died.

I was not in a particularly good state when I got back from the hospital after the beating by Joe with Tara and both Charlie and Melissa, and he was simply standing there at our front gate in a terrible state.

"Danny?" I said, my head aching like anything still from the vicious kicking of Joe's boots.

He didn't look up at him for a few seconds, and terrified I was going to fall got the front door, got me onto the sofa and then rushed out to him saying "Danny?" concerned.

If I hadn't died the following day, those words would have stayed with me right to whenever I should have died.

"Nicole's miscarried".

I couldn't stand without risk of going straight back down again, and he just collapsed into Tara's arms.

Tara looked at me, stunned, wordless. I rang up Frank and both were round in a matter of moments, and after dropping Claire off, who wouldn't leave him alone rushed over to go and get Nicole.

The poor girl was pale and just sat on the sofa, in a state of shock.

The pair had been in Didsbury Village when she suddenly went over and woke up in the hospital when they told both of them the horrible news.

Why he left her alone when they got home, I do not know but there was no way we were going to leave them alone.

"You look terrible, Andy" He sat beside me on the Sofa while Claire and Tara talked to Nicole in the other room.

I don't remember where Frank was.

"I had the misfortune of running into Joe's size 11 Doc Martens before at the Mall"

"Do you want me to go and deal with him?" He chipped trying to sound positive.

"Frank's size 13 feet broke his nose" I tried laughing but failed completely and utterly "I'll be fine" I tried carrying on trying to put a positive spin on things.

What made it worse was that Danny was due back out on tour with his band the day after.

"I can't go and let the guys go" He tried reasoning with me "They need me".

"Nicole needs you even more, don't you realise? Stuff the money m8" I was shocked.

He looked down at the floor, shocked "I can't afford to miss the tour, Andy, I simply don't have the money".

"Don't work about that" I took his hand "I've got a little bit of spare money"

We agreed to come round the following evening and I would get a bit of a further advance from my agent for him to keep them both afloat while he sorted himself out.

The reality was I was dead by the time he came around the following evening.

I have no idea how Tara would have reacted to this double whammy of me dying by the edge of the river, a victim of my kindness and Danny and Nicole's losing their child in the space of twelve hours.

If I had lived longer, I like to think I would have been able to offer some comfort to the madness that would be going on around us instead of making the problem twice as bad.

I have regrets, sure, that I didn't live longer than I did but it saddens me even more that Danny and Nicole's child never made it into the outside world.

It's immaterial what kind of life they would have had, I dare suspect they would have been born into a rocky relationship between Danny and Nicole, with Danny barely there and Nicole struggling all the time.

I know my life finished off earlier than I don't doubt it should have done. Their daughter didn't even get that chance, instead leaving behind nothing but a shadow, rather a fragment of a shadow of a life that could have been, instead finding the door was bolted shut before they could arrive kicking and screaming.

I know in my case for example, all of my books and even that low-budget film I directed when I lived in London may disappear into the graveyard of whereafter out-of-print books and forgotten films eventually go after the world has forgotten about them or has no need for them, but for whoever sees them or reads them will know of the impact, be it little made on this world.

Danny and Nicole's child never got the chance which makes this even more tragic. I know my life was just going in the direction I wanted it to go when I died but their poor daughter haunts me and I dare say will haunt me more than what happened to me next for the rest of eternity and leave this world filled with regrets.

I wish I could say more about that night about Danny and Nicole, I lasted about another hour or so and went to bed feeling battered and blue (which I was) and lay face up looking at the ceiling for hours and hours until I heard them eventually go with Frank and Claire and Tara get into bed with me.

"You, okay?" She cuddled up next to me.

"Not really" I didn't move.

"Poor girl" She didn't add any more.

I didn't know what to say and listened to her nod off to sleep in just a few minutes.

I just lay there for seemingly an eternity unable to sleep almost like I knew what was coming next and there would be nothing I could do to stop it no matter what I did next.

It's a shame or a poetic irony you could argue what happened to both me and their daughter.

I've read somewhere that tragedy like this comes in threes.

I don't remember where.

I hope this is not the case as I dread to think of the effect it could have on everybody, as two tragedies in the space of 24 hours could rip out the texture of any family and that saddens me more than anything else.

I'm told Danny and Nicole's daughter is a beautiful young woman who has taken the trauma of her non-existent life a lot better I dare than what I would have managed that's for sure.

One of the Angels, I guess you can call them, has said she may well want to give it another chance someday of living again.

Me?

They have asked me if I want to live again already but I don't know.

I don't know.

I don't know.

I honestly don't know if I could live again, not after how this last one lived.

I'll not go into the topic of past lives here, but the way I died has left me sitting by the edge of my little ranch in the afterlife looking at the endless sunset haunted by my life from the beginning right through to the end only to have it snatched away when I really could have gone with still being alive, instead of being sat there looking at my life in an endless loop unable to sleep.

Looking back at my life, I know exactly when I was born and can remember every moment from when I was born, and the panic in the doctor's face when they tried delivering me over seven weeks early,

I know now how lucky I was then when it would have been just as easy to lose me and Bobby who was the opposite nearly two and a half weeks early, and my general weakness I had through the first few years at School, before eventually catching up with myself in my 20s.

Being a premature baby certainly in the days when I was a child was not easy when I had several other disabilities that only came to the forefront after I had left home for the first time.

It would be easy to talk about them, but that helped make me what I was when I died I know now and I can see that now when I died collapsing on the riverbank, my heart exploding into a splinter of shadows and the immense journey through time that followed in an endless loop of the very fabric of my full life.

A life I learnt from dying was a journey was just the beginning of what came next, and Life was like opening up the first door to the secrets of everything that comes after.

A life I learnt was a series of memories linked into fragments like looking at the snow falling into winter light to the next day walking across the meadows to where I died each time, I looked at it a little differently from the last time I was there.

Everywhere as if each memory told a different story if I looked at it differently collected into one point at the border point between life and death throwing everything aside to what you expected to happen simply does not happen and takes off in a direction you simply didn't happen.

Death is a funny business in the sense of no loss of life I know now is the same as somebody else's who I may see where I am now, Take for example, my father's father – and grandfather for example. He died in the hospital slowly over a few weeks after suffering a bad fall and was rushed there by my father and uncle after my grandmother rang them both within moments.

I was too young of course to understand and was told by Mother he was ill after falling, and wasn't allowed to go and see him simply getting told, he would be out before I knew it only for his stay in hospital to turn into one week, two weeks, then two months etc and just when it looked like he was going to come out of the hospital, he ended dying in there after close to six months as his body slowly began to shut down and left us all completely heartbroken at the way he died.

This was in complete contrast to my grandmother who less than three months after he died quite horribly died simply in front of her Television with a cold half-drunk hot chocolate next to her on her little coffee table in her sleep and was not discovered for close to a week after her neighbours stopped seeing her, and she stopped returning everybody's calls.

Mother told me later in life, she saw this coming as her father had been the one who paid all the bills, and did almost everything and when he died, she simply went to pieces quite quickly.

My death?

I don't know which I would have preferred out of either of the above, I remember telling Tara only a few weeks before if I were to die, I wish I would die happy and hopefully die in the arms of the woman I loved not to see it dragged out over months or to simply drift away from life after loving the love of my life.

I certainly wouldn't want to die the way I did a good two miles away from where we lived.

There had been issues, sure with both of our families which made life hard for us on several occasions but it wasn't something I would have wished otherwise, no matter whether it was my brother being awkward with his lifestyle choices shall we say, or in Tara's discovery, a jealous, well over-jealous ex, the discovery of a sister she was not aware and a brother who she found out years after she was born was her adopted brother rather than an actual blood brother and who was as complex as his actual music.

And me?

I hadn't had it easy that was for sure rushing around England unable to deal with my own guilt of the way I couldn't handle what happened between me and Tara, and how her own unsubtle background had left her not in a fit physical state to fall in love.

Well, not at that stage in her life anyhow.

Of course, it was my brother, Bobby and his girlfriend later his wife, Paula's fault for drawing us back together whether they planned it or not. (I like to think they hoped we would get back together).

In "Birth" I talked about how she turned up unexpectedly with Paula and Bobby to watch me read from my novel, and I can blame them both for drawing us back together as a couple.

I dare say they didn't expect what happened next between us when the four of us went to the Lloyds hotel across the road, and after they both went, I dare say they didn't expect us both to carry on for hours and then formally get back together as a couple quickly afterwards.

I had dreams for years before we met, I would bump into her somewhere and we would stand there and start shouting at each other in the middle of Chorlton Mall, or I would look at her and look straight forward in hatred and carry on walking.

Of course, the reality was completely different as you may have guessed and once we dealt with the problems that split us in the first place, not expecting what happened next between the pair of us, and despite the fact we've had family all around which are all flawed and I know will stay flawed now I am gone, but hate them? Even Joe after he beat the shit out of me barely a day before I died.

I could have hated him with all my heart, but the reality was I felt sorry for him.

The same also applied to my death.

I couldn't hate anybody over what happened to me there.

I wish I could honestly, but I couldn't.

I wish I couldn't remember the exact details of that last morning right from when I got up, but I do which haunts me like a ghost.

Tara didn't want me to go to work that day not after Marcus beat the shit out of me the day before.

"You should phone in sick after that, they'll understand" I remember her pleading with me as we both watched the girls slowly get up late for college.

God knows what time they had both got to bed the night before, but I suspect they have both been up probably one of Charlie's computer games late again.

Tara was right I know looking back at that last day. I should have stopped in bed. I should have phoned in sick. I should...

She had seen me over a little more than 24 hours previously covered in a pile of blood from her ex who was clearly either completely drunk or on drugs and knew if Frank, her brother-in-law hadn't gotten involved as he did, goodness knows what would happen to me then.

Looking back at things now, perhaps if I had stayed at home and not gone to the office I do not know if I would have died and could have picked up both girls after they finished college.

Because I was known a little bit around the college for my novels, I usually got pestered by somebody or the other outside of the college, not that I was too upset by it.

Perhaps.

"Andy" She begged at the front door for the second time as I stood there slowly heading over to work "You don't have to go to work, do you – you look terrible"

She was right and it haunts me looking back now afterwards.

"They need me in the office" I began "We've got an audit in next week."

"Andy" She looked at me again with almost tears in her eyes.

"It'll only be for a few hours" I reached for my coat "I'll be back just after lunch, I promise. I need to sort out just a little bit of paperwork".

I never saw her again.

I stood there for a few seconds after she left, and I came close to taking my coat back and sitting back down.

I felt terrible, but I didn't. The office needed me for just a few hours, I told myself several times, I could rest when I got back home.

Looking back now, I know I should have simply phoned into the guy's sick.

They would have heard about what happened to me in the mall, and they would have all been asking in their way why had I come in after getting beaten up like I had the day before.

Would I still be alive if I had stopped at home, I don't know looking back now.

I don't know.

I could have still dropped dead just as easily taking the rubbish outside or run over by a car pulling in reverse putting rubbish in the communal bin on the way down to work.

Instead, I just had a normal morning in the office.

All the guys like Tara did back at home no doubt saw how rough I looked when I walked into the office.

I can't remember who said what to me exactly when I walked into the office, but everybody was worried and I had a cup of coffee in front of me on my desk before I had finished taking off my coat, and two chocolate biscuits.

That last morning was uneventful thankfully, a lot more uneventful than I in truth expected and I spent most of it on the phone dealing with a query from a client who we had done work with a few months before.

He had been a good client of ours for some years prior to that, and I know we needed some specific information from him for the audit, and I couldn't ask anybody to phone him up for the information without him either going completely mad at them, or have a total panic attack.

"Hi Paul, it's Andy from Pearsons" I remember beginning.

"Andy," He laughed "How the devil are you?"

I laughed back "We've got the auditors in again next week"

"It's not been a year, has it?" He paused.

I grunted and carried on a few seconds afterwards "Sadly, yes" I paused "Can you provide us with a copy of the payment receipt for the job we did for you on the Buckley Estate for you as I think they are going to ask for it"

He swore under his breath. I couldn't blame him there as I knew that would take some digging up and he said "Okay, give me until tomorrow morning and I'll pop over in the morning for you with it. Ten O'clock okay?"

"Sure, that's fine" I verbally nodded and terminated the call.

Knowing Paul, he would have been there for as close to ten as possible the following morning.

I dread to think what he would have walked into then when he eventually arrived.

After that, Lydia, Kelly's assistant rang up.

Kelly was on holiday in Canada or somewhere visiting her family, so whenever she was away, Lydia looked after her clients including me.

I had met her once the last time I was in London, and she was a polite, petite little blonde, very softly spoken Glaswegian lady, maybe in her early 20s.

She wasn't as good as Lydia, of course. She hadn't been in the business for fifteen years, at least like Lydia had, rather two or three since leaving university, but she had a politeness and calmness that I liked and in time I had no doubt she would have done as well as Lydia and the rest of the agency.

"Hiya Andy" She began when she rang me up.

"Hiya Kelly" I didn't look up from my audit papers.

She went silent for a few seconds. I knew something was wrong and waited for her to catch up.

"They're not happy with the latest draft" She stumbled slightly on her words. "I think they are going to withdraw the contract"

"Have you messaged Lydia?"

"Yes" She paused and I knew from the pause Lydia hadn't responded yet and would be as furious as me when she picked up the email when she did "They've sent over ten pages of alternatives they want you to make"

"Bastards" I swore under my breath. I stopped looking at my audit papers.

I didn't need this, I swore under my breath, I didn't need this I repeated this to myself, not on top of the Audit which was going on.

The book deal I knew was for an awful amount of money, and it was, in fact, the biggest deal I had ever come across. Lydia had done herself more than proud with this deal, and we both knew it, which is probably why Kelly hated ringing me with the news she had.

It wasn't Lydia's fault.

It wasn't Kelly's fault.

It wasn't anybody's fault, just a case of simply bad luck and I sat there looking at the audit and then at the telephone.

The book deal was a lot of money, an awful lot of money, but so were the accountants and the audit which was coming up.

I couldn't let them down, but it wasn't enough and would never, ever be enough but so was the book.

I had been working on the book for close to three years and had gone through four massive re-edits/redrafts and I then saw the stress staring me straight in the face.

It was a lot of money and time on both sides, and it scared me.

No, it terrified me in fact, and I couldn't move away from staring at both the phone and the audit.

Work vs my writing??

Writing vs my work??

Work vs my writing and everything I had ever wanted from the full of my life.

Work? I couldn't move and the rest of the morning flew by, and I don't remember telling everybody I was going for lunch and don't remember walking down Beech Road.

I don't remember crossing the gates at the end of the woods and was then at the edge of the river in just a few moments more.

I hadn't had any history of heart problems, and neither had anybody else in my family, when the pain hit me, I would have screamed if I had the energy but over the following few seconds, it felt like a searing pain was thrusting itself through my chest.

I gasped out, I started to struggle for breath and tried to reach for the gate post in front of me. The pain thrust out and punched out through my chest, spreading out like wildfire in seconds to my left arm. I tried to reach to grab my arm, but I couldn't move as it flew through my body to my neck making it feel like it had locked and then my jaw.

I couldn't speak and felt my stomach turn and began to start sweating from the top of my forehead, then felt my vision begin to blur as the world around me tilted and spun around in pieces.

Did I fall or did I trip on mud or did my body begin to pack up on me?

Had I taken on too much or had the kicking I had taken the previous day from Joe proved to be too much and led the slow trial to my death which was pushed forward by the stress of what had happened to Danny and Nicole's miscarriage and also what was going between Bobby and Paula?

I tried to pull myself back up, tried to call out for help, but my legs wouldn't move neither would my arms. I could hear my heart pounding faster and faster before finally cutting out altogether like it was racing one final small race before finally stopping altogether and it felt like I was sinking, deeper, deeper and deeper into an abyss.

My life began to start flashing before my eyes from when I was born, to being in Siren, to running away and then returning home to when I met Tara again.

I tried to blink but the images began to speed up around me, almost like I knew when I got to the end of the sped-up movie I was going to die and there was nothing upon nothing I could do about it.

Was I already dead?

Had I been dead for several moments?

What was going on?

"Are you okay, mate?" I heard a voice say from the other side of me.

A young couple who I didn't know were around me in seconds.

"Are you okay mate?" He repeated to me, reaching down to me.

I tried to answer, honestly to tell them what had happened to me, but the words wouldn't come as much as I wanted them to speak to them.

"Marc, is he okay?" She, I guess she was his girlfriend, called out stunned in shock slightly further back from him.

"I don't know" He looked at me shocked and then turned back to her "I think he's had a heart attack, have you bought out your mobile phone?"

I couldn't hear her answer, but I could see her in the shadows to call what I think looking back was for an ambulance, but it was too late.

I tried to call out Tara's name to say I was sorry but all I felt was a calmness sink into me, and then was it music?

Was it a harp?

and then was jolted when Marc rushed at me.

"Marc" She called out shocked.

He was inside my pockets before she could finish calling.

"Fuck it, he's dead" He was inside my coat jacket. "He's not going to need this where he is going next".

I couldn't stop him and began to cry helplessly.

"Stop" A voice called out from the other side of him.

"Fuck off" The man wouldn't move.

I knew without being able to look up, it was Bobby.

The man looked at him and swore and tried to hit him.

I heard a punch and saw my bank card fly up into the air.

I don't know what happened to the young couple, did they run?

Bobby stood over me in seconds.

Where he had come from, I never found out.

Was he just walking through the woods?

"Andy" He looked out, his eyes flooded with tears. "Oh my god"

I tried smiling but died in his arms seconds later unable to say anything else further to him.

I know where and when exactly I died, almost as well as I know exactly when and where I was born like it is a circular pattern, begins and ends.

I know it like one of my novels right to the moment like when it rains or snow begins to unexpectedly in June and each moment keeps staring at me in the face, spelling over each moment over and over until it feels like you are looking at another person's life.

An ending that keeps leading back to the beginning like it was a department of truth, the light fading slowly into the darkness

I could hear the faint strains of music again, not just a harp but a symphony of sounds, each note resonating with a part of my soul. It was beautiful, more beautiful than anything I had ever heard. As I surrendered to the music, I felt myself being lifted and carried away.

I tried to reach out to Bobby and could see nothing but his tears as I was slowly led up to the skies.

Life and death, beginning and end.

It all merged into one.

And then there was nothing.

No darkness, no light, just an endless expanse of nothingness.

A void where time stood still, where thoughts ceased to exist. It was as if I had been erased, wiped clean from the canvas of existence. Yet, within this emptiness, a sense of peace washed over me, it was as if I had finally found a home, a place where I belonged.

Was this everlasting light, a story itself leading over the page? Was my life merely a first draft, filled with errors and inconsistencies, waiting to be revised and perfected in a realm beyond comprehension?

Had I spent my whole life wandering around in circles only to realise I was myself a character in a grand cosmic narrative?

Was my ending a reversal leading back to my beginning and everything that lay in the middle?

Or somewhere in between?

Epilogues

Tara

The study was the hardest to clear out Tara found out afterwards after the funeral and not his books which were sprawled out all over their house.]

It used to drive both her and the girls mad but if you asked him where a book was, he would know in seconds or his record of extreme metal, Scottish bagpipe music and whatever the fuck he had bought back from that trip overseas that time.

'Death and horror' she remembered at the time saying it out loud to him in front of the girls 'Is this another of your strange metal records?'

'No' She stopped outside the study she remembered him telling her with an innocent look which always broke her heart before telling her it was a BBC Sounds effect record from 1977 or so which he said many of the effects on it were created using mistreating cabbages.

'Really?' She said in shock turning the lock to herself, remembering the jokey teases he threw at her about how he would play it for her over the following two weeks before he eventually played it one night after they all went to bed, and quietly threw it away not saying much even when Charlie asked what did he think of it just after?

If it had been her, she would have left it at that, but Charlie had just been promoted to Captain of the 4th year girls' football team and wouldn't let it go.

Andy was good, always good with both of the girls she stopped realising he had locked the door and smiled gracefully with her as he did with Melissa, her other daughter over almost everything. If he had been the girl's blood father, he may well have reacted a little differently, but she breathed out slowly thankfully was nothing like Joe.

Thankfully.

Joe, she remembered reaching inside her pockets for the keys was a mistake which she let drag on for a heck of a lot longer than it should have done, but she had the girls, and she kept telling herself it would get better.

It never did.

Stepping into the study, she looked around at the scattered papers all over the place and would likely have been on with things the way things were with Marcus if Andy hadn't stumbled back into her life, she owned him for that she knew giving both her and the girls the 11 years they had had and the adventures they had all had.

She smiled sitting on his chair facing the early sunrise, remembering the countless hours they had spent together in this room, sharing dreams and aspirations, happiness and tears, a present and future obliterated by the past, papers scattered all over the floor like a smudged jigsaw, a whirlwind of ideas and passions that had shaped their lives covered in sunlight instead of the darkness which haunted her heart.

Melissa and Charlie

Melissa initially wouldn't go to the funeral.

'No, I can't do it" she told her twin sister in her room.

"Yeah, me too" Charlie sat down next to her on her bed.

"Really?" Melissa looked at her stunned. She was used to Charlie being the strong-willed one, the one who was not afraid of anything right from when she took over as the School Captain when she was 13. Unlike her, who was more interested in her art brush.

"Yeah, he wouldn't want us to go if we felt uncomfortable doing this"

"At least, he wouldn't have to hear any of those bloody awful records of his now, would we?" Melissa tried smiling.

Charlie got up and walked towards the record for a few seconds and Melissa thought for a few seconds she wasn't going to answer her. She was the one out of the pair of them that was known for long pauses in her conversation, not Charlie.

Never Charlie.

"That's true", She didn't move. "They were awful that's for sure"

"Do you remember that time he put on that Bagpipes and the electricity went off" Melissa giggled.

"I am convinced Mum flicked the electricity switch off to stop it" Charlie cut in.

"Did she hate those records that much?"

Charlie nodded. "She would never tell him of course"

Charlie carried on.

"I can't believe he's really gone," Melissa whispered, her voice barely audible.

Charlie nodded; her eyes filled with sadness. "It still doesn't feel real, I went into his study yesterday, mum had left the door unlocked".

"Was it still a bloody mess?"

"Yes, there were papers everywhere. Mum said they are trying to get all of his papers to sort out his novel"

A gentle knock interrupted their thoughts.

Melissa looked at Charlie.

"Girls" Tara walked in, in tears. They both hugged her.

"Mum" Charlie began.

"I know," Tara said "I can't believe it"

Melissa couldn't answer her.

"Andy loved you both dearly like they were his own daughters"

Melissa and Charlie looked at each other. They knew Tara was right. They owed it to Andy to be there, even if it was difficult.

"He hasn't got either of those bloody awful records lined up at the church, did he?"

"I hope not" Tara tried smiling as they walked down the stairs.

Bobby and Paula

Bobby was the last one to arrive at the funeral. In fact, he was so late with his wife that Paula wasn't sure if he was going to show at all.

'You, okay? She grabbed his hands when he sat down.

'No, not really' He shivered.

He nodded at Tara, who was a few seats away from them both, unable to say anything else, and then seeing what pain he had gone through simply started crying again.

She stood up and saw Claire, her sister was there before she got there, and Claire's husband, Frank, was sure his name had come up to her and spoke to her in a much gentler way than she was used to seeing, "He was a good man" and she saw he was sitting there shivering like a ghost.

Her limited experience of Frank had been of a roughneck with a heart of gold, and she knew he and Bobby weren't on good terms after a big fight a few years before which Frank gave Bobby a good kicking, but she looked at him and could see he was right.

"I'm sorry, love" She re-grabbed his hand.

"He died in my arms, Paula" Bobby whispered under his breath "I felt the life drain right out of his body"

Andy had been a good man, she remembered when he came back for that book reading, she remembered when she met those years before, but haunted by his past, and like Bobby, she was delighted when he got back together with Tara, but this, she looked at his coffin, it was just bloody cruel.

He was 49 years old, she thought to herself, 49 bloody years old and died of what appeared to be a heart attack.

She looked again at Bobby and told herself she couldn't tell Bobby to calm down here. He and Andy hadn't been close for years after he got back together with Tara, but he had always been nice to her, even frog-marching him down to the wedding after he got stupidly drunk the night before and tried running off.

"You poor bugger" She looked again at the Coffin and stood up when they led the service outside to the graveyard.

Bobby wouldn't leave her arm, and Danny, Tara's brother whom she hadn't met before was stood there carrying the coffin outside with Frank and a few other young men.

There was a French-sounding much younger woman standing there who had a young girl she hadn't met before, and it was all too much until Charlie, one of Tara's daughters came up to her outside the church.

"Auntie Paula" She hugged herself "Thanks for coming, I know Andy err. Dad would have loved you being there"

She laughed back at her, but as Charlie hugged her, she felt a pain in her stomach.

"You, okay?" Claire, Tara's sister stood next to her almost out of nowhere.

"No, I'm fine" She tried laughing it off.

"No, you're not" Claire looked at her "How far gone are you?"

Pregnant, the words came into her head, and she just looked shocked at Bobby.

After Death

After the funeral, Tara returned home to find the door to the study wide open.

"Didn't you lock the door, mum?" Charlie stood behind her.

Tara stood there for a few moments unable to say anything before she hurriedly locked the door again "I'm sure I did"

Melissa grabbed her hand as she reached over "No, Mum"

Tara looked at her surprised.

"It could be a sign, mum" She began to shiver.

Tara stopped and began to open the door slowly.

Papers were all over the floor.

"Is this a sign?" Charlie stepped slightly forward "Is Andy trying to tell you something?"

"Yes" She bent down "It's time to get his final book organised"

Bonus Segment:

Toward the end of the fourth draft of this novel, I ended up attending a novel writing workshop where the tutor came up with an interesting idea, why don't we rewrite a segment from our novel but just do it from a different perspective?

    Death, even though it is a book about well, Death is a book of love and forgiveness really, the piece which follows next I wanted to look at it from the other side of the emotions of the main character and reverse what a lot of the main characters were nature wise, and thought it would make an interesting afterthought to conclude this book.

Footnote

Going to your own funeral, I have to say was a surreal process or a play I no longer had a role in right from when they brought out your body in a coffin. First of all, behind the carriers was my wife, Tara who stood there weeping into a crumpled handkerchief and then turned around to our two daughters, Melissa and Charlie who were both stood there looking disinterested in the full bloody process.

Melissa, the eldest of the two girls by about fifteen minutes, stared at her phone, occasionally glancing up with a look of boredom. Charlie, the younger one, kicked at the floor, shifting her weight from one foot to the other, her eyes glazed over. They had always been Tara's daughters, never mine only getting worse the further our marriage carried on.

The priest's eulogy was kind but impersonal, a list of achievements that barely scratched the surface of who I was. I stood there looking at them watching Bobby, my brother put a comforting arm around our mother then walked over to Tara and she cried into his arms, and I thought for a moment he was going to kiss her.

Was my death just an inconvenience to him, an opportunity to step into my place? With one last look at Tara's performative sorrow and the girls' disinterest, I felt a dark, bitter realisation: I had been an outsider in my own life, and now, even in death, I was being replaced.

Did Tara care for him or was she really grieving me?

Did the girls ever have any feelings or were they masking it?

I didn't know her, my story with them was over, but their story, it seemed, was just beginning, and I feared the role my brother would play in it.

Even in death, I was little than a footnote to my life.

Andy N is the author of ten poetry collections, including the books 'From the Diabetic Ward Volume 1' and 'Changing Carriages at Birmingham New Street' and is the co-host of Chorlton's Spoken Word night 'Speak Easy'.

He also does ambient music under the name of Ocean in a Bottle and does the music for the band' Polly Ocean' and runs / co-runs Podcasts such as Spoken Label and Not the TV Guide.

His debut novel is 'Birth'. (Described as a charming coming of age Novel about the birth of a Writer – available on Amazon). His second novel 'Death' will be out in February 2025 and the second album by Polly Ocean will follow in the Spring / Summer 2025.

His links can be found at:

https://linktr.ee/andynartist

Also by Andy N:

Step into the mesmerizing world of "Birth," the debut novel by Manchester-based poet, podcaster, and ambient musician, Andy N.

Delve deep into the psyche of a young writer as this extraordinary tale offers a poetic, sad, and often hilarious portrait of his coming-of-age journey as his creativity is almost literally dragged out of him into the beginning of his journey as a poet, into fronting a five-piece acoustic band, and so much more.

In this captivating narrative, the reader is taken on a profound exploration of the writer's upbringing, skillfully woven with evocative prose that casts a spellbinding charm. "Birth" is a novel where the young writer's world is painted with a palette of feelings, where joy and sorrow dance hand in hand, and humor is found even in the darkest corners.

"Birth" is more than just a novel; it is an ode to the human spirit, a celebration of the written word, and a testament to the resilience of the creative soul.

So, open the cover and step into the world of "Birth," where the boundaries between reality and fiction fade, and the heart of a young writer beats with unyielding passion. What happens next is a testament to the magic of storytelling and the boundless potential of a pen.

DEATH

"Departing from the personal introspection of his earlier poetry collections, 'Changing Carriages at Birmingham New Street' marks the poignant culmination of poet, podcast host, and ambient musician Andy N's poetic journey. Like a masterful tapestry, Andy weaves a narrative that resonates with the expressive essence of Paul Auster's prose and the heartfelt drama reminiscent of Hugo Williams's 'Dock Leaves' before taking it far differently.

"Changing Carriages at Birmingham New Street," is a symphony of emotions touching upon the exquisite fragility of our shared experiences travelling over towns and cities. with each poem resonating like a chord of truth, readers are invited to traverse the landscapes of their own emotions, memories, and aspirations.

"Changing Carriages at Birmingham New Street" is a literary sojourn over a childhood revisited by a first love that returns over twenty years later and quietly chokes away that resonates deeply within the chambers of the heart of memories spread out over a lifetime well beyond the final page. It is a book waving at you from a distance, the potency of narrative, and the eternal beauty of sadness that find a home within us.

After being in the same job for over ten years and then facing unemployment when neither of his following roles proved a good match, Andy N knows firsthand the challenges of navigating the job market in an ever-changing world. In *Beyond the CV*, his second book of non-fiction, he shares his honest and inspiring journey of what happened to him offering practical advice and valuable and personal insights of how he pulled himself back from the edge.

Originally told in a series of columns on his Substack page, now expanded to include unreleased material, Beyond the CV is a series of articles reflecting this journey which covers his initial struggles obtaining interviews, dealing with rogue firms, cancelled job fairs with no notice and how to use job agencies.

Beyond the CV also covers suggestions on how to re-edit your CV when you are struggling, how to choose between two job offers you receive at once, and then what you do when said job choice is withdrawn, this book covers everything you need not to give up.

Told with a touch of humour and wisdom rarely seen in said market, *Beyond the CV* is your guide to a more fulfilling and successful career as well as a guide not to give when it looks like you may never work again.

Beyond

www.ingramcontent.com/pod-product-compliance
Ingram Content Group UK Ltd.
Pitfield, Milton Keynes, MK11 3LW, UK
UKHW030953240225
455493UK00011B/912